Please return this book on or before the date shown
above. To renew go to www.essex.gov.uk/libraries,
ring 0845 603 7628 or go to any Essex library.

Essex County Council

Luca was everything she shouldn't want. He was dangerous.

He was a man who was used to people doing what he wanted them to, and he was willing to take whatever measures were necessary to make it happen.

They would come to a coparenting arrangement that suited them both, but that was it. That's all there could be.

Claire looked up to notice Luca was watching her as he held their child. His gaze flicked over her casually, and yet she could feel the knot in her belly tighten. She wasn't misinterpreting this. Luca made it plainly clear that he was attracted to her, as well. It might just be a negotiation strategy to soften her up, but when he looked at her that way, it almost made her feel like resistance was futile.

Luca was a man who got what he wanted. What would she do if he decided he wanted her?

The CEO's Unexpected Child

ANDREA LAURENCE

First published in Great Britain 2016
By Mills & Boon, an imprint of HarperCollins*Publishers*
1 London Bridge Street, London, SE1 9GF

Large Print edition 2016

© 2016 Andrea Laurence

ISBN: 978-0-263-06629-6

Our policy is to use papers that are natural, renewable and recyclable products and made from wood grown in sustainable forests. The logging and manufacturing processes conform to the legal environmental regulations of the country of origin.

Printed and bound in Great Britain
by CPI Antony Rowe, Chippenham, Wiltshire

Andrea Laurence is an award-winning author of contemporary romances filled with seduction and sass. She has been a lover of reading and writing stories since she was young and is thrilled to share her special blend of sensuality and dry, sarcastic humor with readers. A dedicated West Coast girl transplanted into the Deep South, she's working on her own happily-ever-after with her boyfriend and their collection of animals.

To Those Battling Cancer—

You never expect the *C* word and when it shows up, your whole life turns upside down. Things that seemed so important are suddenly trivial compared to getting through this disease. I can't even imagine the full scope of emotions that go through a person as they face that uncertain future. My wish is that this book provides you a welcome distraction and gives you hope for a happy ending of your own.

One

"I don't care, Stuart. I'm not letting a total stranger just take my daughter from me."

Claire Douglas's lawyer, Stuart Ewing, patted her on the hand. He had a grandfatherly way about him, an easygoing attitude that belied the fact that he was a courtroom barracuda. She had a lot of faith and money invested in the man, but that didn't mean she wasn't terrified deep down.

"We'll work something out, Claire. I just need you to keep your cool when we go in there. Don't let your emotions get the best of you."

Claire frowned. Keeping her emotions in check

was not exactly her specialty. She'd been bombarded with emotions over the past two years. Her life had become a roller coaster from the moment she found out she was pregnant. After years of failed fertility treatments, it had been their last chance. That moment had been the highest of highs.

Her husband dying in a car accident when she was five months pregnant was the lowest of lows. Especially the painful revelations that followed it. The birth of her daughter had been the only thing that pulled her out of that dark place, giving her a reason to be joyful and live her life again.

But she'd never expected this. The disclosure of the mistake they'd made at the fertility clinic had changed her whole life. It had made her a millionaire, and at the same time had threatened the stability of her small family.

"Mrs. Douglas? Mr. Ewing? They're ready for you." The receptionist at the front desk gestured to a set of double doors that led to a conference room.

There, Claire presumed, waited the man who was trying to take her child and the lawyer he'd hired to help him. She felt her stomach roll, threatening to return the coffee and bagel she'd forced down her throat that morning.

"Come on, Claire," Stuart said, pushing up from the waiting-room chair. "Everything is going to be fine. You're not going to lose your daughter."

Claire nodded, trying to act calm and assured, though she was anything but. There were no guarantees. They were marching into a room where Edmund Harding was waiting for them. He was the kind of lawyer every billionaire in Manhattan had on speed dial. Harding had such a level of prestige and influence that he could probably get the courts to do anything he wanted.

Scooping up her purse, she forced her trembling hands into tight fists at her sides and followed Stuart into the conference room.

The room was elegant and intimidating, with a large rectangular glass table that cut it in two like a blade. There was no question that it divided everything into their side and their opponents' side. There were plush leather rolling chairs lining the table, but at the moment all of them were empty.

Claire's gaze drifted to the large, floor-to-ceiling windows on the left side of the room. A man stood in front of it, looking out over Central Park. She couldn't make out any of his features, just the hulking shape of his broad shoulders and narrow waist. The man was tall, his arms crossed over his chest. He emitted an intense energy that Claire picked up on immediately.

"Ah, Mrs. Douglas," a voice called. "Mr. Ewing, please have a seat."

Claire turned toward the voice and found a man on the other side of the room. He was gathering paperwork in his hands and carrying it to the table. The man had a certain studious look about him that convinced her that he was the infamous Edmund Harding. That meant the man by the window had to be…

"Luca, we're ready to begin," Edmund said.

As Claire settled into her seat, the man at the window finally turned. When he did, Claire was very glad she was already sitting. The face that regarded her was like a Florentine masterpiece of the Renaissance. He had a square, clean-shaven jaw and high cheekbones that looked as if they were carved out of marble. Dark brows hovered over narrowed eyes that crinkled at the edges.

Those eyes ran over Claire for a moment, then turned away, disinterested. He strode to the conference table and sat beside his lawyer.

This was the father of her child?

She almost couldn't believe it, and yet her daughter's dark curls and olive complexion certainly hadn't come from her.

"Before we begin, can my assistant bring anyone anything? Water? Coffee?" Edmund asked.

"No, thank you," Claire said quietly.

"Coffee, black," the man across the table demanded. No niceties, no please or thank you. He seemed very much to be the kind of man who was used to getting what he wanted.

He wouldn't get his way this time. Claire was determined not to let this man get his hooks into her daughter. He didn't even know Eva. How could he possibly get custody of her?

The assistant brought Luca a mug of black coffee and silently disappeared as quickly as she arrived.

"Thank you for coming today," Edmund began as the door clicked shut. "We asked to meet with you in person because we feel as though our prior communications aren't having the impact they should. Mr. Moretti is very serious about pursuing his joint custody filing."

Being served with papers that said a stranger was demanding custody of her daughter had nearly floored her. When she had learned the truth about the mix-up at the fertility clinic, a part of her had hoped that the biological father would be disinterested in Eva. She found out quickly that was not going to be the case.

"Don't you think that filing was premature?" Stuart asked. "He hasn't even met the child, but he thinks he should have joint custody?"

"He would've met his daughter weeks ago if your client had cooperated with our requests. We had no choice but to do something Mrs. Douglas couldn't continue to ignore."

The two lawyers continued to argue, but Claire found her attention was drawn to the silent force sitting across from her. While his lawyer did all the talking, Luca Moretti leaned back in his chair and studied Claire. His dark hazel eyes ran over every inch of her. She did her best to hold still, not wanting to squirm or show any sign of weakness in front of him.

Instead, she focused on studying him just as closely. It was so easy to see pieces of him in Eva. When her daughter was born, Claire had been confused by the baby they handed her, with the head of dark, curly hair. Claire had dark honey-blond hair. Her husband, Jeff, had light brown hair. Neither was olive skinned nor had a cleft in their chin, but Eva did.

But all her confusion and worry disappeared the moment she looked into her daughter's gray eyes. She fell in love that instant, and no longer cared what Eva looked like because she was perfect. For all Claire knew, Jeff had Spanish or Italian blood he'd never told her about.

The doubts hadn't arisen in her mind again until the clinic called three months later. They'd informed her that their last vial of sperm was due for destruction in three months if they didn't use it. They hadn't opted to pay the lifetime storage fees because they'd intended to use it all fairly quickly.

The call confused her because they'd used their last dose when they conceived Eva. That information had raised red flags, and it wasn't long until they discovered the truth—her husband's sperm had a number transposed on the paperwork and another client's sperm was used instead.

Luca Moretti's, to be exact.

The thought sent a chill through her. The man had never touched her and yet a part of him had been inside her. What was a man like Luca doing at a fertility clinic, anyway? Putting himself through college by selling sperm for cash?

Every inch of his body, from his broad shoulders to his hard jaw, screamed the kind of masculinity she hadn't been exposed to in a very long time, if ever. With the right look, Claire was certain he could make a woman's ovaries explode. If a man like Luca needed the services of a fertility clinic, a lesser man didn't stand a chance with his own progeny.

And yet, he was there. When the news broke, Luca had focused his attention on the fertility clinic. He'd sent Edmund after them and before Claire knew it, the clinic was begging to settle out of court and keep the scandal quiet. She had instantly gone from a comfortable middle-class woman, to someone who didn't need to work another day in her life.

But then Luca turned his legal bulldogs on her. Claire wouldn't back down, though. She didn't care if it cost her every penny of her settlement battling in court. Eva was her baby. It was hard enough trying to deal with the revelation of her daughter's paternity. She was still trying to work through her anger and confusion about Jeff's death. How could she tell Jeff's parents that Eva wasn't their biological granddaughter? She had a lot on her plate already. She didn't need Luca coming out of nowhere and making demands about *her* child.

"There's got to be a happy medium," Stuart said, pulling her attention back into the conversation.

"My client isn't open to negotiating any terms that don't involve providing him with visits with his daughter."

"*My* daughter." Claire spoke up with all the force she could muster. She felt Stuart's hand covering hers, trying to calm her, but it wasn't going to help. "Eva is my daughter. I'm not just going to hand her over to some stranger. I don't know anything about this man. He could be a serial killer or some kind of pervert. Would you just hand over your child to a stranger, Mr. Harding?"

Edmund was startled by her outburst, but the sound that caught her attention was the snort of laughter from the man beside him. It was the first noise Luca had made since he demanded his coffee. When she turned to look at him, she noticed a sparkle of interest in his eyes and a hint of amusement curling a corner of his full lips. He was no longer just studying her, he actually seemed…intrigued by her.

"I can assure you that my client is no criminal, Mrs. Douglas. He is the CEO of the nation's largest family-owned Italian restaurant chain, Moretti's Italian Kitchen."

Claire turned away from Luca's intense stare. It was unnerving her, and this was no time for her to be compromised. So, he was a hotshot restaurateur. Good for him. But what difference did that make when it came to his character? Success didn't make him a saint. "So you're presuming that rich businessmen can't be murderers or child molesters? I counter that they just have better lawyers."

"My client is willing to cooperate to soothe your concerns, Mrs. Douglas. We're not the bad guys here. We're just trying to ensure that Eva is in Mr. Moretti's life. We welcome you to have a background check conducted. You won't find anything questionable. But when you don't find the skeletons you're looking for, you're going to have to let him see Eva."

"And if Mrs. Douglas doesn't cooperate?"

Claire held her breath, waiting to see what they would say. Would they push her or back down until their court date?

"Then," Edmund explained, "we stop playing nice. I'll file an emergency visitation motion to compel access to Eva and let the courts decide. You can be certain the judge will give my client even more time with his daughter than we're requesting. It's your choice, Mrs. Douglas."

So this was Claire Douglas.

Luca had to admit he was surprised. Her name had been on his mind and crossed his desk a hundred times since the mix-up came to light. He didn't know what he was expecting the widowed Mrs. Douglas to look like, but young, slender and blonde had not been on the list. It had taken everything he had to hold his composure when he turned from the window and saw her standing there.

Her practical gray suit clung to every delicious curve and almost exactly matched the shade of her eyes. Her honey-colored hair was twisted back into a professional bun at her nape. He wanted to pull out the hair pins and let the blond waves tumble over her shoulders.

The longer he sat watching Claire, the more curious he became about her. How had a woman so young become a widow? Was she always this uptight, or was it just because she didn't like him? He wanted to run his thumb between her eyebrows to smooth the crease her serious frown had worn there.

It made him wonder if their daughter looked more like him or her. Did she have Claire's porcelain skin and pert nose? Did her ears turn red when she got angry the way her mother's did? The furious shift in Claire had immediately caught his attention. There was more fire in her than the bland gray suit would indicate.

"Can they do that?" Claire asked, turning to

her lawyer. She looked completely panicked by the thought of Luca having access to their child.

Their child.

It seemed so wrong for him to have a child with a woman he'd never met. Luca hadn't even given any serious thought to having a family. He'd only stored his sperm to make the doctors and his mother feel better. He hadn't actually expected to use it.

But now that he had a living, breathing child, he wasn't about to sit back and pretend it didn't happen. Eva was probably the only child he would ever have, and he'd already missed months of her life. That would not continue.

"We can and we will." Luca spoke up at last. "This whole thing is a mess that neither of us anticipated, but it doesn't change the facts. Eva is my daughter, and I've got the paternity test results to prove it. There's not a judge in the county of New York who won't grant me emergency visitation while we await our court date. They will say when and where and how often you have to give her to me."

Claire sat, her mouth agape at his words. "She's just a baby. She's only six months old. Why fight me for her just so you can hand her over to a nanny?"

Luca laughed at her presumptuous tone. "What makes you so certain I'll have a nanny for her?"

"Because…" she began. "You're a rich, powerful, unmarried businessman. You're better suited to run a corporation than to change a diaper. I'm willing to bet you don't have the first clue of how to care for an infant, much less the time."

Luca just shook his head and sat forward in his seat. "You know very little about me, *tesorina*, you've said so yourself, so don't presume anything about me. Besides, even if I have a nanny, it doesn't matter because Eva is my daughter, too. I'm going to fight for the right to see her even if all I do is pass her off to someone else. Like it or not, you don't get any say into what I do when I have her."

Claire narrowed her gaze at him. She definitely didn't like him pushing her. And he was pushing her. Partially because he liked to see the fire in her eyes and the flush of her skin, and partially because it was necessary to get through to her.

Neither of them had asked for this to happen to them, but she needed to learn she wasn't in charge. They had to cooperate if this awkward situation was going to improve. He'd started off nice, politely requesting to see Eva, and he'd been flatly ignored. As each request was met with silence, he'd escalated the pressure. That's how they'd ended up here today. If she pushed him any more, he would start playing hardball. He didn't want to, but he would crush her like his restaurants' competitors.

"We can work together and play nice, or Edmund here can make things very difficult for you. As he said, it's your choice."

"My choice? Hardly." She sniffed and crossed her arms over her chest.

The movement pressed her abundant bosom up against the neckline of her jacket, giving him a glimpse of rosy cleavage. Her blush traveled lower than he expected. It made him want to know exactly how much lower.

"Mr. Moretti?"

Luca jerked his gaze from Claire's chest and met her heated stare. "I'm sorry, what?"

"I *said*, you have my hands tied. You aren't even listening to me. How can we negotiate when you aren't listening?"

Luca swallowed his embarrassment, covering it with the confident, unaffected mask he usually wore. It had been a long time since he'd lost his focus during business discussions, much less because of a beautiful woman. Apparently, he had been working too much and needed some companionship so he didn't lose his edge. "And how are we to negotiate when you refuse to move from your position? You won't listen to anything that isn't just the way you want it."

"That is not—"

"Claire," her lawyer interrupted in a harsh whisper. "We need to consider what they're offering."

"I don't want to consider it. This whole thing

is ridiculous. We're done here," she said, pushing up from her seat to stand.

"That's fine," Luca said, sitting back in his chair. Time to turn the screws. "I think you'll look lovely in orange."

"Orange?" Claire asked, some of her previous fire starting to cool.

"Yes. Prison jumper orange to be exact. If the judge orders visitation and you don't comply, you could end up in jail. That's fine with me, really. That means I'll get full custody of Eva."

"Sit down, Claire," Stuart said.

Her brave facade crumbled as she slipped back down into her chair. Finally, he'd gotten through to her. The last thing he wanted to do was to send a young mother to jail, but he would. He was not the kind of man who bluffed, so it was a wise time for her to listen.

Claire sighed and leaned forward, folding her delicate, manicured fingers together on the glass table. "I just don't think you understand what you're asking of me. Do you have nieces or nephews, Mr. Moretti?"

Did he? He was from a big Italian family. With five brothers and sisters he had more nieces and nephews than he could count on two hands. The newest, little Nico, was only a few weeks old. "I do."

"And how would you feel if one of your sisters was in my position? If her husband died and she was blindsided by the news that he wasn't the father of her child? Then to be forced to hand over your niece to a stranger because of circumstances outside her control?"

That made Luca frown. He ran the family enterprise with his brothers by his side. His whole life revolved around Moretti Enterprises. Family—blood—was everything to him. That's why Eva was so important. Regardless of circumstances, she was family. The idea of letting Nico go off with someone they didn't know was unnerving, even if that man had the right. Perhaps he needed to change his tactics with Claire. Bullying would not change her mind any more than it would change his sister's mind.

"I understand how hard this must be for you.

Despite what you might think, Mrs. Douglas, I'm not keen to snatch your baby from your arms. But I do want to get to know my daughter and be a part of her life. I'm not backing down on that. I think you will be more comfortable with the entire situation if you get to know me better. A lot of your concerns about me and how well I'll care for Eva will be gone if we spend some time together. By that I mean time with all of us together, so you can be there for every moment and be more at ease with my ability to be a good father."

Claire's frown started to fade the more he spoke. "Do you mean like playdates? I appreciate what you're trying to do, but it's going to take a long time for me to be comfortable if we're just spending an hour or two together every Saturday afternoon. How much can I learn about you during the occasional walk through the park?"

Luca shook his head. "Actually, no, that's not what I mean. You're right. It's going to take more time than that."

"What are you suggesting, Mr. Moretti?" her lawyer asked.

"I'm suggesting we both take a little time away from our jobs and spend it together."

"Tiptoeing around your penthouse apartment?" Claire asked.

He shrugged. He hadn't given much thought to where or how. "Why not?"

"I would prefer more neutral territory, Mr. Moretti. I won't be comfortable in your home, and I doubt you'll enjoy the mess a baby and all her things can make in your fancy apartment. You're not going to be happy coming to Brooklyn, either."

"Okay. What do you think about us taking a vacation together? Renting a beach house or something?"

"Luca, I'm not sure that's such a good—"

"I'm listening," she said, interrupting Edmund's complaint. Claire's delicate brows then drew together in confusion. "It sounds nice, but how long of a vacation are we talking about, here?"

If they were going to do this, and make it work, they couldn't skimp. She was right; a few hours here and there wouldn't get them anywhere. He needed to get to know the mother of his child, to bond with his daughter and to make Claire at ease with him and his ability to care for Eva. That would take time.

"I think a month ought to do it."

Two

"A month?" Claire was stunned. "Mr. Moretti—"

"Please, call me Luca," he said with a smile that made her pulse quicken in her throat.

That was a dangerous smile. It was charming. Disarming. Combined with his movie star good looks, it was enough to make her forget that he was the enemy, not a potential paramour. She almost preferred that he return to his cold, businessman expression.

"*Luca*, I have a job. I'm a curator at the Museum of European Arts. I can't just leave for a month, especially on short notice."

"Do you think it will be easy for me to simply turn over the reins of my family company for a month? It will be a hardship for both of us, but it has become very clear that it is a necessity to make this work. We need time away, just the three of us, to get comfortable with one another. Don't you think Eva's welfare is worth the sacrifice?"

Nice. Now Luca was the good guy and Claire was the one being unreasonable because she wouldn't do whatever it took for her daughter. "Of course she's worth the sacrifice. My daughter is my whole life."

"Then what's the problem? The way I see it, our court date with the judge is in six weeks. After spending four of those weeks together, perhaps we can come up with an arrangement that makes both of us happy and can present that to the judge."

Claire felt Stuart squeeze her knee beneath the table. She didn't have to look at her lawyer to know that he liked this idea. No one wanted to go up against Edmund Harding in court if they could avoid it. Going to see the judge with both parties on the same page would make things easier on everyone. Including Eva.

That was the thought that won her over. Her boss wouldn't be happy, but he would understand. He knew what she had been going through the past two years. He'd be the first to tell her she deserved a vacation. Maternity leave was hardly a break. That was just a six-week introduction to the hard life of a single mother.

"Okay. If you agree to take the emergency visitation filing off the table, I'll agree to your proposal."

Luca nodded slowly and gestured to his lawyer. "Okay. I'll make the arrangements for a location."

"I'd prefer it not be too far away," Claire said. "Long trips with a baby are difficult, and I'm not sure I'm ready to take her on a plane."

"I have an old friend from college who has a place on Martha's Vineyard. Would that suit you?"

Claire tried not to react. Martha's Vineyard

was the summer playground of the rich. Until recently, she'd been solidly middle class, and a vacation locale like that had always seemed out of her reach. The sudden increase in her checking account balance hadn't changed her mindset along with her tax bracket. "That would be suitable," she said, coolly.

"Very well. I'll speak to Gavin and make sure it's available. How long will you need to prepare for the trip and arrange the time off?"

It was Monday. At the best, she could leave this weekend. "I'm not sure, but it will take a few days."

"I'll give you my contact information. Let me know when you find out, and I'll have a car sent to pick you up."

"That's not necessary. I can arrange my own transportation." Claire was never the kind of woman who sat back and let people take care of her. Not Jeff, and certainly not Luca. She had the capacity and the money to handle this herself.

"Ridiculous. We'll ride together and start getting to know each other as soon as possible."

Claire clenched her jaw. He spoke as if everything was law. It made her crazy. She had to pick her battles, though. If he wanted to send someone all the way out to her brownstone in Brooklyn to pick them up, then fine. "Very well. Are we done here?"

Luca's lips twisted into an amused smile. "We are."

Good. Claire was in desperate need of getting out of this room. The spacious conference room closed in on her the longer Luca stared at her. Those dark hazel eyes had the slightest hint of gold twinkling mischievously in them. He seemed to look right through her, seeing all the secrets and shame she was desperate to hide.

Picking up her bag, she pushed up from her seat and turned her back on Luca Moretti. She needed some distance between them. She wanted to breathe air that wasn't scented with leather and the spice of his cologne. Claire moved with purpose out of the conference room, exiting Edmund's law offices with Stuart on her heels. She didn't stop until she was standing on the sidewalk, looking at the traffic buzzing down Lexington Avenue.

Claire took a deep breath and felt the muscles in her neck and shoulders finally start to loosen. It wasn't just what he saw in her. It was how he made her feel. Luca lit a fire inside her that licked at her cheeks and made her think about the needs she'd ignored for longer than she could remember.

When she and her husband decided to have a child and it didn't happen easily, sex with Jeff became a chore. Mechanical. When that didn't work and they went to the clinic, it was even worse. Desire and arousal went out the window with sterile rooms and medical procedures. Their relationship changed as their failures became all they could focus on.

It was no wonder Jeff strayed.

Claire had been so wrapped up in getting pregnant, and then obsessed with preparing for the baby's arrival, she didn't notice anything was wrong. Jeff was working later, going on more business trips, but a lot of people worked long hours. Even she did from time to time, especially when a new exhibit was getting ready to open at the museum. But she also ignored the fact that he took a shower the minute he got home, the distant look in his eyes and the complete disinterest in physical contact. She was so adept at justifying every red flag that if his mistress hadn't died in the car with Jeff when he wrecked, she might never have accepted he was having an affair.

It had taken time to come to terms with the truth, but knowing that her relationship with Jeff would've ended no matter what had helped her cope with his death. She had lost her husband long before that night. If Jeff had lived long enough for the truth about his infidelity to come to light, they probably would've divorced. And if by some miracle they had fought through the rough patch, finding out that he wasn't Eva's father would've been the end. His ego never could've taken a hit like that.

Realizing all this had been a major blow to her confidence in her ability to make good choices. She had thought Jeff was the perfect man for her and she'd been wrong. She'd thought a baby would help give her what she was missing from her life and her marriage, and it wasn't. She loved Eva more than anything and didn't regret having her, but a baby hadn't been the answer to their problems. In the end it made them worse.

Being attracted to Luca Moretti was another bad decision. Even as she could feel his gaze raking across her skin, she knew it was a terrible idea. And yet, she hadn't felt that alive in years. He hadn't even touched her and she'd reacted to him like no other man before him.

"Claire, are you okay?" Stuart came up behind her, placing a soothing hand on her shoulder.

"Yeah, I was just ready to get out of there."

He nodded, looking out at the passing cars. "Let me take you to lunch." They turned and started walking down the sidewalk. "All things considered, I think it went okay today. Edmund's not filing an emergency visitation petition, so that buys us some time. He's willing to work with us to come up with an agreement before

we go to the judge. It isn't going to get any better than that."

"Yes, but it cost me four weeks of my life."
She would pay more than that for Eva and her
well-being, but she was still a little shell-shocked
from everything that just happened.

"Claire…it could be worse. You're going to
spend a month at a beach house on Martha's
Vineyard."

"With Luca Moretti," she pointed out. Somehow that made it seem like less of a vacation
and more of an obstacle course she needed to
survive.

"So what? Between you and me, I think you
need the break. Get out of New York, sit on the
beach and breathe in the sea air. It's beautiful up
there this time of year. It's early in the season,
but that means it won't be too crowded or hot.
Let Luca take care of Eva under your watchful
eye and be grateful for the time off. How does
Japanese food sound for lunch?"

This trip sounded good on paper, but she was
certain that the reality would be very differ-

ent. She'd barely made it through a half hour with Luca with both their lawyers present. What would she do when she was alone with him for a whole month?

Luca strolled down Park Avenue, heading toward his apartment. He could've called a car to pick him up, but he needed the walk. It helped him focus, or in this case think about something else. It took about ten blocks before he could get the sound of Claire's sigh from his mind. Her steel-gray eyes haunted him.

He hadn't expected to have a reaction to her like this. He didn't want to, either. That woman had been nothing but difficult, despite how politely he'd tried to handle this mess of a situation. And yet, he couldn't help pushing her buttons just to see the fire in her. Under that prim suit and tightly wrapped bun was a passionate woman, he was certain of it.

Of course, what did it matter? He was pretty sure that Edmund would advise him strongly not to get romantically involved with Claire. He knew it was the smart thing, but Luca didn't always follow the advice of others.

Turning the corner, Luca finally reached his building. Standing beneath the dark green awning was Wayne, the second-shift doorman.

"Good afternoon, Mr. Moretti. You're home early today. I hope everything is okay."

Luca smiled at the doorman who had worked here longer than he had owned the apartment. "No worries, Wayne. All is well. I'm actually home a little early to start planning a vacation."

"You, sir? I don't think you've had one of those since you moved in."

Was it that obvious that he was a workaholic? "Probably not. I've been working pretty hard lately. I'm going to be gone for a month, though, up to Martha's Vineyard if all goes to plan. Will you let the building manager know I'll be away? I'll need my mail and packages held until I return."

"I will, sir. May I ask if you're doing something fun on your trip?"

The thought of the rosy blush running over

every inch of Claire's porcelain skin instantly came to mind. That could be fun. Or it could be four weeks of bickering by the beach. "Maybe. It depends on how it goes. I certainly hope so."

Wayne pulled open the shiny brass door and took a step back. "Well, I hope you enjoy your time away. You've certainly earned it, sir."

"Thanks, Wayne."

Luca crossed the marble lobby floor to his private elevator. He smiled as he pressed the button that would take him up to his apartment. Claire thought she knew so much about him, but she was wrong on several counts. For one thing, he didn't live in the penthouse. He lived on the tenth floor of his building. The penthouse apartment was just too large for his needs. His apartment had three bedrooms and an unused maid's quarters. That was more than enough.

When he'd purchased the place a few years ago, he was pretty certain he would live there alone for the rest of his life. Despite the fact that he had bent to the will of his doctors and his mother as a teenager by storing the potential for future children at the clinic, he had no intention of ever using it.

A wife and a family were the furthest thing from Luca's mind. He'd found that people who lived through what he had reacted one of two ways—they were either desperate for family or terrified by the idea of it. Luca fell into the latter category, although he hadn't always felt that way.

The doors of the elevator opened to the marble foyer of his apartment. He unlocked the door, stepping into his living room. Luca slipped out of his coat and headed for his study. There, he poured himself a finger of Scotch and settled down in his favorite leather chair.

As the oldest of six kids, he'd presumed he'd have a family of his own someday. He enjoyed the camaraderie and the chaos of his childhood home. Then, at age sixteen, those presumptions went out the window when his whole life was derailed by an unexpected illness. The illness turned out to be testicular cancer. The treatment for his cancer was aggressive—surgery and several rounds of chemotherapy and radiation. The majority of patients who went through the treatment were sterile when it was over. Although the idea of it was mortifying, he'd made several donations to be frozen at the fertility clinic for the future. His mother paid the clinic big money for them to hold on to it for as long as Luca might be in need of it.

Luca knew when he was doing it, however, that he would be storing, but not using it, forever. Despite assurances to the contrary, he knew he was a damaged commodity. At any time, the cancer could come back or spread. Physically, he wasn't the complete man he'd once been. Plastic surgery had corrected the aesthetics, but he knew the truth. He couldn't knowingly go into a relationship with a woman knowing that he was limited in what he could offer her.

And he was limited. He knew that in his heart. The one time a woman had claimed to have given birth to his child, he'd let himself get his hopes up. His whole family got their hopes up. When the miracle baby turned out to belong to someone else, everyone was disappointed, including the baby's gold-digging mother, Jessica. He had always been adamant about using protection, just for safety reasons, but after that he was almost militant. He didn't want another woman to even get the idea that she could have his child.

Sipping his drink, he looked around his study. It was a part of his perfect bachelor pad, decorated with masculine touches of leather and dark wood. The shelves were lined with books he'd never read. On one wall was a framed portrait of the world, reminding him of all the places he'd never been. He'd gone from being a child, to a cancer patient, to a college student, to a CEO. That didn't leave room for much else.

It was just as well that Jessica's baby hadn't been his. Even if he wanted a family, he didn't have time. From the day he was born, he'd been groomed to take over Moretti's Restaurants. His great-grandfather had started the company eighty years ago with a small restaurant in Little Italy. By the time his grandfather took over, they had another restaurant in Brooklyn and one in

Queens. It snowballed from there. His father's goal of having a Moretti's in every state had been achieved not long after Luca was born.

After he got sick, his mother had home-schooled him from the hospital to help him keep up with his studies while he received his treatment. When he graduated from high school in remission, Luca went to Harvard to get his business degree and started working at the corporate offices with his father. His MBA earned him the title of vice president, and his father's retirement two years ago had turned the reins over to him entirely.

Luca had put his own stamp on the empire by diversifying their restaurants. Not everyone had the time for a long, sit-down Italian feast. He started a fast-food Italian chain called Antonia's, after his mother. That had exploded, becoming one of the fastest growing chains in that market.

Overseeing this monster took all the time he had. And he liked it that way. When his life was so full, he didn't miss the family he was lacking.

And now, suddenly, he found he had a family he never expected—one that had been confirmed as actually being his. Thankfully the apartment could accommodate Eva, in terms of size and space. There would need to be some childproofing and redecorating, but that was the least of his worries. The harder part would be seeing to it that the rest of his life could accommodate his newfound daughter, as well.

That started with this trip. The first thing he needed to do was to call his old friend Gavin Brooks. He and Gavin had met at Harvard and hit it off immediately. Like Luca, Gavin was the heir to a family empire of his own—Brooks Express Shipping. They both understood what it was like to have that kind of pressure on their shoulders. The difference was that Gavin had managed to run BXS *and* have a family. He and his new wife, Sabine, had two small children, including a baby girl named Beth, who was only a few months older than Eva.

Perhaps Gavin could offer Luca more than just a vacation house. He could use some advice, as well.

Reaching for his phone, he dialed Gavin's number.

"This can't really be Luca Moretti calling me," Gavin answered abruptly. "I mean, that's what my phone says, but my friend Luca never calls me."

Luca sighed. "That's because your friend Luca works too much and is never sure when he can call without waking up your kids."

Gavin laughed. "It's a crapshoot. Jared is an early bird and Beth is a night owl. We pretty much never sleep around here. How are you, Luca?"

"To tell you the truth, I'm overwhelmed." It was nice to be able to talk to someone who truly understood what his days were like. He and Gavin were members of an elite club of young, successful businessmen in Manhattan.

"The restaurant business giving you trouble?"

"No. Work is fine. I called because I need your help for a more…personal matter."

"I thought you didn't have personal matters."

"So did I, then it got dropped in my lap."

Oddly enough, this was another situation that Gavin could sympathize with. He didn't learn about his son, Jared, until the boy was almost two years old. "I need your help, Gavin."

"Sure, anything. What is it?"

"Okay. If I tell you something, will you promise not to tell anyone?" At this point, Luca couldn't risk the news of Eva's existence getting out. He'd worked hard to keep the lawsuit under wraps so far.

"Sounds serious," Gavin said. "I'll keep it to myself."

"Thanks. I'm trying to ensure this whole situation stays quiet for the next few weeks, primarily because of my family. You know how they are. I need to deal with all of this without their interference."

"Your cancer has come back," Gavin said in a grave tone.

"No, thankfully. I've actually found out that I'm a father."

"A father? For real this time?"

In retrospect, Luca had wished he'd kept the

situation with Jessica quiet until he knew for certain. He'd never expected her to lie about it. He should've known when he saw the look on her face after Edmund demanded a paternity test. As though he'd just take her word for it. "Yes, this time it is tested and established to be my child. I have a daughter named Eva."

"But wait," Gavin argued. "I thought you couldn't…"

"I can't," Luca confirmed. "But I had some sperm frozen before my treatment. There was a mix-up at the clinic and a woman ended up pregnant with my child instead of her husband's."

"Holy hell. What are you going to do?"

"Well, first I sued the crap out of the clinic. Now I'm trying to negotiate custody terms with the mother. I can assure you it hasn't been easy. She's not happy about all this."

"I can imagine her husband isn't that happy, either."

"I'm not sure if it makes all this easier or more complicated, but her husband is actually deceased. Apparently he was in a car accident when she was pregnant."

"I thought my situation with Sabine was complicated, but you take the cake, Luca."

"Thanks. This brings me to the favor. I've proposed that all three of us spend some time away to get to know each other. She's not very confident in my ability to take care of a baby and I've got to convince her everything is going to be all right."

"Why don't you just tell her that you helped raise your younger siblings and have spent time with a dozen nieces and nephews? The last time you came over, you handled Jared like a pro."

That was a good question. "I doubt she would believe me. She's a feisty woman, and to tell you the truth, it's more fun to aggravate her."

"It sounds like this vacation might prove a little dangerous. Where are you going?" Gavin asked.

"That's where you come in. I was hoping that we could stay at your beach house for a couple weeks. A month, actually."

Gavin only hesitated a second before he answered. "Sure thing. We're not going back up there until after Memorial Day. But why wouldn't you stay at your family's place in the Hamptons?"

That had occurred to him. They had a huge place in Sag Harbor where the family liked to gather. But it was too big. And at this point, he didn't want to run the risk of crossing paths with his family. "To do that, my mother would find out. As it is, I've got to feed my brother an excuse to run the business while I disappear for a month. I will tell them, and soon, but I need to spend time with Claire and Eva without Mama circling like a shark around her granddaughter."

Gavin laughed. "Fair enough. When are you going up? I'll have the place cleaned and the pantry stocked before you arrive."

"I'm not exactly sure. We both have to make arrangements with work, but I'm hoping in the next week."

"So, four weeks in a beach house with the woman you accidentally impregnated and the child you've never met? And the woman doesn't like you, at that."

Luca sighed. "That pretty much sums it up."

"Well, good luck to you, man," Gavin said. "I'll have a bicycle messenger bring you the key tomorrow. And just in case, I'll have the cleaning company hide anything breakable."

Three

Claire paced nervously around the living room of her Brooklyn brownstone. After her meeting with Luca Moretti and his lawyer, things had moved faster than she'd expected. Her supervisor at the museum had been understanding about her situation. The exhibit she'd been working on the past few months had opened the week before and everything was going smoothly. It was actually the perfect time for her to take a vacation, so he'd practically shoved her out the door. With no excuses, she'd called Luca and told him that she could leave as soon as Saturday.

Then her conscience got the best of her. Despite their battles over the past few weeks, Luca had yet to meet Eva. She doubted that the ideal place for their first meeting was the back of a hired car on their way to Martha's Vineyard. She could hear the voice of her lawyer in her head, telling her to play nice. Before she could stop herself, she'd invited Luca over Thursday night.

He should be there any minute.

At the moment, Claire was practically buzzing with nervous energy. Since she'd gotten home, she'd barely held still. She'd already cleaned downstairs, fed and bathed Eva and put her in her footie jammies so she'd be ready for bed when the time came. Eva was currently lying on her jungle gym mat, babbling at the brightly colored lion and monkey toys dangling overhead. She could lie there for hours, contently slobbering on a plastic ring striped like a zebra.

The sound of the doorbell nearly sent Claire leaping out of her skin. She didn't know why she was so anxious about having him over. It wasn't just the idea of a billionaire in her home, although that was intimidating enough. It was a billionaire with an influence on how she raised her child. Would he think their home wasn't good enough? Would he argue her neighborhood was unsafe? That she wasn't providing well enough for Eva? Any of those things could tip the scales in court to Luca's favor.

Truthfully, she didn't know how he could complain. She and Jeff had bought and restored this beautiful brownstone a few years earlier. It was in a safe, trendy part of Brooklyn with great schools. Even then, it wasn't the Upper East Side. She didn't have a doorman or co-op board to keep the riffraff from moving in nearby.

Claire forced her feet across the parquet floors to the front door. She glanced through the peephole, seeing Luca waiting impatiently on her front stoop. Just a glance at him, knowing he was about to step into her home, sent a shiver through her whole body. She wasn't quite sure if she was excited or terrified by the prospect. She unlocked the door and opened it as she took a deep breath to push all those feelings aside. "Good evening, Mr. Moretti," she said.

He smiled and stepped through the doorway. He had a pink chenille teddy bear in his arms and a more relaxed expression on his face than at the lawyer's office. "Please, I told you to call me Luca," he insisted.

She knew that was what he wanted, but she didn't like the idea of it. It was too casual, too intimate. She preferred to keep some formality between them, at least for now. It felt as if it would make things easier over the next four weeks if she had that emotional buffer, even as the scent of his cologne was making her pulse spike in her throat. Ignoring his request, she shut the door behind him and returned to where he was waiting for her in the foyer.

Luca took the opportunity to study her home, admiring the architectural details she'd worked so hard to preserve. Claire much preferred her view of him at the moment. He was looking very handsome tonight in an expensive navy suit that was tailored to highlight his broad shoulders and narrow hips. He'd paired it with a blue-and-brown geometric tie that seemed to capture the same shade of milk chocolate as the waves of his hair.

Chocolate waves of his hair? Claire squeezed her eyes shut for a moment to rid the image from her mind. Why was she cataloging his good looks, anyway? That was not what tonight was about. Or any night from now on. Luca might be Eva's father, but it didn't happen the old-fashioned way. Thinking of him like that was dangerous while their custody arrangement was still up in the air. She couldn't afford to make a mistake when it came to Eva and her welfare.

"I wanted to thank you for inviting me over tonight," he said as she took his coat and hung it in the entryway closet. "I realize this is difficult for you."

Claire forced a smile. "It was the least I could do," she said. "After all, you're treating us to a month at the beach." *Or trapping us with you for a month at the beach.* Same difference, she supposed.

"You can thank the CEO of Brooks Express Shipping for that, actually. We went to college together. It's his beach house we're going to be staying at as a favor to me."

"Of course it is." She chuckled dryly. Apparently rich guys just hung out together. Claire hadn't been around many superwealthy people, but she wasn't surprised to think they all knew one another. They certainly weren't spending their time with people like her. At least until now, when he had to.

With a shake of her head, she turned away from him and led Luca out of the entryway and into the open expanse of her living room. "Well, this is Eva," she said, holding her arm out in front of them to where she was playing.

Luca turned in that direction and froze in place the moment his eyes fell on their daughter. For a powerful CEO who was always in control of everything, he seemed to be at a total loss in the moment. He didn't take a step toward Eva; he just kept watching her from a distance.

Claire decided to help by easing him into his

new role as father. She walked across the room and scooped Eva up off the floor. Cuddling the baby in her arms, she turned back to Luca. "Look who's come to visit, Eva. You have a new friend here to see you."

Eva turned her head to look at Luca, her big gray eyes taking in the new person and processing it however her little baby brain operated.

Luca finally loosened up, leaning in to the baby with a wide, friendly smile. "Hello, *bella*."

Eva rewarded him with a slobbery grin, showcasing her two new bottom teeth. She was usually a little shy with strangers, but she seemed to warm up to Luca immediately. When he reached out to stroke her chubby little arm, she grabbed his finger and held on tight.

"You've got a good hold of me, don't you? How about I trade you my finger for a fuzzy bear?" Luca held up the pink bear and Eva's eyes immediately shifted to the new pretty.

She let go of his finger and reached out for the soft toy with a cry of delight. Luca handed it over to her, laughing as she immediately put the bear's ear in her mouth.

"Everything is a teething toy these days," Claire said. "Thank you for the gift."

"It's long overdue," he said with a touch of sadness in his voice.

Claire noted it, feeling guilty for her role in that delay. Her lawyer had been right; none of this was Luca's fault. He just wanted to be a part of his child's life, and he deserved to be. As much as she didn't want to admit it, the time together at the beach would make this situation workable for both of them. They needed it. "Would you like to hold her?" she asked.

"Yes," he said with a touch of excitement in his gold and brown eyes.

"Here we go," Claire said in the soft baby voice she used for Eva. Lifting her off her chest, she moved Eva over into Luca's waiting arms. He scooped her up like a professional. Perhaps it was beginner's luck.

"You are a sweet little thing," he said, cooing

at his daughter. "I'm going to be wrapped around your little finger before too long, I can tell."

Claire took a step back to let Luca have his moment with Eva. After a few minutes, he moved over to her couch and settled Eva on his knee. It didn't take long for her to see that he was right. Luca was completely enamored with his daughter and they'd only just met. She understood. The minute she'd laid eyes on Eva, she was totally and completely in love. Luca looked just as she imagined she did then.

The reality of the moment was like a fist to her gut. She stumbled back a little, bracing herself against the doorway to the kitchen. Luca didn't notice. He only had eyes for Eva. As a new father should. It was the inescapable realization that she should've had this moment months ago, in the hospital with Jeff at her side, that threw her off balance. She should've gotten to watch her husband hold their daughter for the first time with that same look of wonder and adoration on his face.

Instead, her moments in the hospital had been

bittersweet. She'd cradled her baby, alone in her room, and cried. They were tears of joy, tears of sadness, tears of loss. She wouldn't have that moment with Jeff because he'd gotten himself killed while he was out with his mistress. She wouldn't have that moment with Jeff because in the end, Eva wasn't even his daughter.

How had her life gone so far off the rails? Claire had done everything right her whole life. She'd graduated at the top of her class, going to college on an academic scholarship that left no time for boys. After school, she'd married the safe guy who would love her and care for her and their family. Jeff hadn't been the exciting choice, or the man who made her heart race and her insides melt, but she thought he was a stable, responsible man who would make a good father. She'd made all the right choices and did everything her family had expected her to do. And yet, everything had gone wrong.

Watching Luca on the couch with Eva, she saw nothing but sharp contrast between him and Jeff. It wasn't just the difference between Luca's darkness and Jeff's All-American good looks. It was a difference on the inside at a biological, maybe even cellular, level.

She'd spent almost no time with Luca at all, but she reacted to him like no other man before. There was an intensity in the way he watched her that got under her skin and made her cheeks turn flame hot. Everything from his commanding presence to his sharp sense of style caught her attention. Even the smell of him was enough to send an unwanted spike of need through her.

Luca was everything she shouldn't want. He was dangerous. Not in the traditional sense, but she knew she had to watch herself around him. He was a man who was used to people doing whatever he wanted and was willing to take whatever measures were necessary to make it happen. He also seemed like the kind of man who left a trail of broken hearts in his wake. Claire was determined that she wouldn't be one of those women no matter how he made her feel.

They would come to a co-parenting arrangement that suited them both, but that was it.

That's all there could be. Claire would shelve any attraction she had for Luca, and maybe in time she would find a more suitable man to be in her life. Suitable hadn't done her much good the last time, but she wasn't about to throw caution to the wind because Jeff decided to stray. He was just one man with his own issues to cope with.

Claire took a deep breath to center herself and looked up to notice Luca was watching her as he held Eva. His gaze flicked over her casually, and yet she could feel the knot inside her belly tighten. She wasn't misinterpreting this. Luca made it plainly clear that he was attracted to her, as well. It might just be a negotiation strategy to soften her up, but when he looked at her that way, it almost made her feel like resistance was futile.

Luca was a man who got what he wanted. What would she do if he decided he wanted her?

Two days later, Luca rang the doorbell of Claire's brownstone and waited for her to answer.

"One second!" he heard her shout from the depths of the house. A pounding of footsteps got louder as it came across the hardwood floors to the door.

"You can take these bags and the playpen," she started as she whipped open the door, then stopped cold. "Luca?" She flushed that becoming rose color and covered her mouth with her hand. "I'm sorry. I thought you were sending a driver."

Luca shook his head. He occasionally used one around town to simplify the issues of parking and traffic in Manhattan, but he wanted some privacy and control over how today went. They'd need a car at the beach, and he certainly didn't want a chauffeur loitering around and interfering on their time together. He was fully capable of driving them and actually looked forward to it. He didn't get out of the city as much as he'd like these days.

"I changed my mind." Luca reached down and picked up the bags she had closest to the door. "I'll go put these in the car."

She nodded at him, still not quite recovered from his unexpected appearance. "I've got Eva's car seat here. It will take a few minutes to install it."

"That's not necessary. I have one in the car, ready to go."

Claire frowned at him, but Luca simply turned away and headed down the steps with her bags. He knew he shouldn't enjoy surprising Claire, but he did. She made far too many presumptions about him, and he liked shattering them one by one. As he loaded the bags into the back of his Range Rover, he noticed Claire approaching the car with Eva in her arms. Without saying a word, she opened the back door to investigate the car seat.

She wouldn't find any flaws with it. It was a top of the line model for Eva's age and weight. She was facing the proper direction with all the correct support. It was installed per the manufacturer's specifications. He even added a little mobile that hung overhead from the handle to occupy her while they drove.

Luca didn't say any of that, though. He simply loaded the bags, returning to the house to pick up a few more before waiting on the sidewalk for her judgment. "Will it suit?" he asked at last.

Claire turned to look at him with a sort of befuddled expression on her face. "Yes, it's perfect."

"Don't look so surprised, Claire. I manage a billion-dollar corporation. I can buy and install a car seat."

Her mouth dropped open in protest. "I didn't— I mean, I don't think that—"

"Are there any more bags that need to go?" he asked, saving her from herself.

"No, that's all of them. I'll put Eva in the car seat, and then I'll lock up."

From there, it wasn't long for them to get on the road. Once they got out of the city congestion and onto I-95, it was a smooth, albeit longer, drive. He'd been tempted to book a charter flight out of the heliport, but he knew better than to spring something like that on Claire. She said she didn't want to fly with Eva, and that meant she certainly wouldn't want to take a helicopter.

Claire spent the first part of the trip in the back with Eva. When they stopped for a break and some food, Eva had just fallen asleep, so Claire moved to the front. They passed the time chatting about his restaurants and her exhibits at the museum. By the time they drove off the ferry onto Martha's Vineyard, Luca was anxious to be there already.

"Finally," he said as he turned into the driveway and stopped to let both of them get a good view of the house. It was a two-story gambrel-style home with strong Dutch influences on the design. It had gray shake siding with white columns and a deck that extended off the second floor. It was charming for a beach cottage. He pulled up beside the front walkway and they got out of the car to investigate further. "Well, what do you think?"

Claire's mouth was agape as she took in the house, then turned to admire its views of Katama Bay and the Atlantic Ocean beyond. "It's beautiful. And huge. I can't believe this is just for us. Your friend doesn't need it for a whole month?"

Luca shook his head and opened the back of the Range Rover to start unloading. "Gavin works as much as I do. He bought the place so they could spend some time here in the summer. This is early season for the Vineyard, so he wouldn't be up here for at least a month anyway."

Claire returned to the car to unlatch Eva's carrier and take her toward the front of the house. Luca followed with a piece of luggage and the keys to the front door. He unlocked it, swinging the door open for her to go inside ahead of him. They stepped into a small den area with a fireplace and an office. To their left was a staircase. "Gavin says the main living area and master bedroom are upstairs to take full advantage of the views."

They climbed the stairs ahead of them until they revealed an open concept living area. It really was a stunning place. It had arched white ceilings with wooden beams and windows that gave floor-to-ceiling views of the bay. The furniture was soft and comfortable with the rustic sort of country charm that city people gravitated to while on vacation. While someone in Manhattan wouldn't think of having a pillow with a rooster on it in their trendy Greenwich Village loft, it was somehow more acceptable out here.

Claire wandered through the large, bright living room to the kitchen that was big enough for a large family to pile in and cook a feast. Six barstools lined the kitchen island, with copper pots hanging overhead. Beyond it was a dining area with French doors that opened out onto the deck and showcased the view of the water.

"I'll be right back." Luca headed downstairs and made several trips to bring all the bags inside before parking the car in the garage. By the time he came back upstairs, Claire had Eva out of her carrier and perched on her hip. They were standing on the deck, enjoying the sunshine and letting the cool spring breeze blow over them.

Luca wanted to join them, but he was hesitant to interrupt this moment between a mother and her child. There was an expression of absolute joy on Claire's face as she looked down at her baby. Her dark gold hair whipped around in the wind, the sunlight making her porcelain skin almost glow. She looked like an angel standing there in her sundress. He felt a tightness in his chest as he watched her cradle his daughter and point out birds flying overhead.

Learning of Eva's existence had been a shock, but until a few days ago, she'd been more of an idea than a reality. Seeing Eva for the first time had changed everything. When he held her in his arms, he felt something flip inside of him. A protectiveness was roused in him, almost instinctual in its ferocity. After only a few moments together, he would've done anything for his little girl.

It surprised him after suppressing the idea of a family for so long. There was a part deep inside Luca that had still wanted children, but he had avoided finding out if it was a possibility for him. Somehow it was easier to avoid the doctor and not know whether it was off the table than to get tested and know for certain that he had only two frozen chances at biological fatherhood.

Make that one chance, now that one of the samples had been used to create Eva. It was a mistake, malpractice at best, but at the same time it was hard to be angry about it. He'd been sleep-walking through his days, working hard to fill the void in his life, then boom—he had a daughter. Nothing else seemed quite as important as doing whatever he could to keep Eva happy, safe and in his life.

"How many bedrooms are there?"

Claire's voice roused him from his thoughts. He hoped she hadn't noticed him staring at her so intently. "Four. The master suite is to the left off the living room. There are three other bedrooms downstairs."

Claire looked around, awkwardly shuffling her feet as she studied the house. She probably wasn't sure how they were going to work out the arrangements here. Obviously they wouldn't be sharing a room, as much as he'd like to. They were here together as a family, but also to become friends and soothe her concerns about him caring for their daughter. She might be the most alluring woman he'd laid eyes on in a long time, but sex would most certainly complicate their already complicated situation.

"You and Eva should take the master," he said. "Gavin said there's a crib in there because they got the place not long before their daughter, Beth, was born. There's also plenty of room for the playpen and all of Eva's things there." Luca opened the door to the master suite and gestured her to go inside ahead of him.

"Are you sure?" she asked as she stepped inside and surveyed the room with its cheery yellow walls and iron king-size bed. There was a crib and changing table along one wall and a large dresser along the other. "We'll be just as comfortable downstairs."

"Nonsense. This is perfect for you." And it was. The room suited Claire as though it was made for her. Elegant and cheerful, comfortable and effortless. Claire was all that and more. Her beauty was natural, not forced like that of so many other women. She wore just enough makeup to highlight her features, not disguise them. Her clothes looked comfortable, but stylish. Even the scent of her was perfection—like vanilla and cinnamon. It all came together into a distracting and enticing package.

It didn't stop at looks, either. Driving out here, he was impressed by how intelligent and articulate she was. Working at a museum with a degree in art history, she could just as easily discuss impressionist pieces as ancient Egyptian tomb paintings. He hoped their daughter would be as beautiful and smart as her mother. He doubted he could've picked a better woman to have his child if he'd done it himself. The Fates worked in mysterious ways.

The Fates? His mother's superstitious ways were creeping into his thoughts today. With a dismissive shake of his head, Luca went back out to the living room and started bringing Claire's bags inside. "I'll let you get settled in. I'm sure you could use a nap or something after that long drive."

Claire chuckled and settled on the edge of the bed with Eva. "I doubt I'll get a nap, but maybe there will be some quiet tummy time in our future."

He nodded and slipped from the room. Luca stomped down the staircase to the first floor. Once there, he took a deep breath and exhaled Claire's scent from his lungs. If only his thoughts of her could be expelled so easily.

Grabbing one of his bags, he went into each bedroom, selecting the one the farthest from Claire. He dropped the bag on the floor at the foot of the bed and flopped down onto the queen-size mattress. The room was tidy, with blue walls and distressed furniture. In the end it didn't really matter. All he needed was a bed and space away from Claire to keep a clear head.

Four weeks was a long time to be alone with her here. With the longing she stirred inside him with only a glance, it would feel even longer.

Four

The morning light shone through the window and roused Claire from her sleep. She yawned and stretched, feeling luxuriously lazy for not setting an alarm. She could get used to this vacation thing. For the first time in a long time she felt well rested. She'd slept like a rock last night. She hadn't done that since before Eva was born.

Wait a minute... Eva!

Shooting up in bed, Claire looked over to the crib. If the alarm didn't wake Claire up, the baby usually did, so if she was still sleeping, something was wrong with Eva. Her eyes scanned the unfamiliar crib, but there was no baby to be found.

"Eva?" she called out with an edge of panic in her voice.

Claire whipped the blankets back and leaped from the bed. A quick search of the crib and the surrounding area confirmed what she already knew. Eva was missing. "Eva!" she shouted again, throwing open the door of the master bedroom and skidding into the living room. She came to a sudden stop, not quite sure she could believe what her eyes were seeing.

"Good morning. Are you hungry?"

Luca was standing in the kitchen with Eva perched on his hip. Together, they were cooking breakfast. The billionaire CEO was mixing pancake batter while playfully gumming at her infant's fingers and making yummy sounds. Luca looking so casual holding her daughter was a surreal sight after their tense conference room showdown. Was this the same man who had threatened her with prison time? "We've been enjoying our morning, haven't we, *bella*?

We had a bottle and coffee out on the deck and watched the seabirds, and then we decided to make pancakes for breakfast."

She was happy to find Eva safe, but she didn't appreciate the fright he'd given her. Luca's brows drew together. "Claire, are you okay?"

She didn't answer him. Marching across the living room, she took Eva from his arms and cradled her to her chest. Then, and only then, could she respond to Luca. "Please don't do that," she said.

"Do what?"

"Take her without telling me."

"You mean take her like she's my child and care for her as a father would do?"

Claire frowned at him. He might technically be her father, but he hadn't earned the right to just wander off with Eva without her permission. Her daughter barely knew him. "The point of this trip was so that I could get comfortable with you handling Eva. It's been less than twenty-four hours and I can assure you that I'm not comfortable yet."

"I'm sorry," Luca said, coming around the kitchen island with a mug of coffee in his hand. "I get up early, so I came and got her so you could sleep. It defeated the purpose to wake you up and ask if you minded. Would you like some coffee? I made this cup for you, but again, I didn't ask permission first, so you may not want it."

Claire ignored his sharp tone. He was annoyed, but she didn't care. It was far too early for him to start ignoring boundaries. Being temporarily under the same roof didn't turn their situation into some family sitcom. Of course, neither did her snapping at him.

"Sure," she replied quietly, still a little off-kilter from her scare and not entirely pleased with how she'd handled all this in that state. "Thank you."

Luca set the mug on the counter within her reach and turned to the kitchen. With his back turned, Claire did a quick assessment of Eva and found her to be fed, changed and clean. She seemed happy and not at all concerned to be away from her mother with a strange man. Claire had obviously underestimated Luca when it came to caring for children. He knew more about it than he let on in their previous discussions.

"Do you want bacon?"

Claire turned back to Luca. He seemed to have cast aside their little skirmish and refocused on breakfast. "That sounds great." She slipped onto one of the stools at the kitchen counter to watch him work at the range. The in-control businessman appeared to have stayed back in Manhattan and in his place was a man enjoying his vacation. He was wearing a blue T-shirt and flannel plaid pajama pants with bare feet. His hair was slightly messy, and morning stubble lined his sharp jaw.

She imagined that this was a sight few people outside his immediate family got to see. She liked it. More than she wanted to admit. She wondered what his rough stubble would feel like against her cheek. Against her thighs...

Claire squeezed her eyes shut for a moment to

send that sensation out of her mind. She wasn't allowed to snap at him, then fantasize about him a moment later. That was craziness.

When she reopened them, she focused on Luca's cooking. Even in his pajamas, he moved around the kitchen with purpose and fluidity. Luca certainly knew what he was doing. For some reason that surprised Claire. There was a lot about this man that wasn't what it appeared. "I knew you ran restaurants, but I never thought about whether you could actually cook," she admitted.

Luca flipped a pancake, then looked at her with a disarming smile. "In my family, food is life. All our family gatherings revolve around the meals we make together in the kitchen. Once a kid is old enough to peel a potato, they're put to work helping with Sunday suppers."

"Do you have a large family?"

Luca chuckled and flipped over another pancake. "Yes. I'm actually the oldest of six kids. My father is the oldest of five. When we all gather together with the cousins and spouses, there's easily forty or fifty of us."

"Did you help with caring for your siblings?"

He nodded. "Have I surprised you with my ability to handle an infant without completely melting down?"

Claire twisted her lips into a guilty smile. "Yes. I'm ashamed to admit it."

"In addition to my siblings, I have a dozen nieces and nephews that I see from time to time. I have cared for my fair share of children of all ages. Eva is in good hands, I assure you."

"Why didn't you say that at your lawyer's office?" That would've significantly reduced her stress level over this decision. She still didn't want him taking Eva without her permission, but knowing she wasn't the first baby he'd held made a difference.

Luca shrugged. "You made incorrect assumptions about me and I let you. Now that we're here—as you mentioned a moment ago—we can get to know each other as we are, not as others perceive us to be. You'll find most of your concerns are unfounded." He slid four perfectly golden pancakes onto a plate and added a few crispy pieces of bacon on the side. He placed the plate in front of Claire.

"That's a ton of food!" she exclaimed as she eyed the plate-sized pancakes.

"Well, that's the only problem I have in the kitchen. I don't know how to cook for two people. I cook for an army or not at all."

Claire couldn't even imagine having that much family. She had almost none. Jeff's family had been her own for many years and now… Eva was really all she had. She scooped the baby off her knee and put her into her high chair so she could eat. After she snapped on the tray, Luca put a handful of Cheerios out for her to pick up and nibble on while they had breakfast.

"What about you?" Luca asked as he made his own plate. "What is your family like?"

Claire frowned into her coffee mug. "Nothing like yours," she said. "I'm an only child. My parents were only children, as well. I didn't really grow up around our extended family. My father traveled with his job, so it was really just the three of us my whole life."

"And now?"

It seemed like a simple question, and yet it wasn't. Claire had family, and yet she didn't. It was a strange limbo to be in. "And now, it's really just Eva and me. My father had a heart attack and died when I was in college. My mother remarried, and since I was grown and gone, her life became more about her new husband. I don't see or talk to her very often because she lives in San Francisco now. I married Jeff not long after she moved, so I didn't notice the absence. His family was really good about including me for gatherings and holidays even before we got married. They were my family for many years, but now I've lost all that."

Luca settled beside her at the counter with his plate and coffee. "You mean they haven't included you since your husband died?"

Claire shrugged. "It's not that simple. His death was hard on us all. And the circumstances made it that much more awkward for everyone. I don't think they know what to say to me."

Luca looked at her with concern in his dark eyes. "May I ask what those circumstances were?"

She took a moment to butter her pancakes and pour maple syrup over the top. Claire had told this story enough times now that it shouldn't bother her anymore, but it did. The truth never got easier to take. "My husband died in a car accident with his mistress. He told me he had to go out of town on a business trip, but he was really with her. I would never have even known the truth, but they went off the road and hit a tree, killing them both. The police seemed to think she was…distracting him, somehow. I didn't have the heart to ask them why they thought that.

"I was five months pregnant at the time, after years of trying to have a baby," she continued. "It's hard to lose someone you love and yet be angry at him at the same time. There's so many emotions tied up in Jeff's death for me and for everyone else. I just don't think his family knew how to face me after that. Whenever they came to see Eva, his death hung over our heads like a dark cloud. And now they don't have to face it anymore. I haven't heard from his parents since I told them about the clinic mix-up. Apparently both Eva and I are disposable since we're no longer their blood relatives."

Spitting out the last of it, Claire shoveled a large bite of pancake into her mouth. There was something about admitting her pathetic story to Luca that made it worse than telling anyone else. She didn't want him to see her for the lonely, pitiful woman she felt like when she told her sad, sordid tale.

"That means it's just you and Eva now."

It was a statement, not a question, but Claire nodded as she chewed nonetheless. It was true. Eva was everything she had, which was why she'd fought so fiercely not to lose her daughter to a mysterious father. "Someday, I hope to have another chance at marriage and maybe another child if it's at all possible. But if that never happens, I'm thankful that I have Daisy, Eva's nanny. She's like family to me."

Luca's brow went up. "A nanny? After all the grief you gave me about handing Eva off to someone, you have a nanny?"

"It's not the same," Claire argued. "I didn't want Eva handed off and ignored. Daisy just watches Eva while I'm at the museum. When I get home, Daisy leaves and it's just the two of us. She gets one-on-one attention and care, and I thought that was better than putting her in day care while she's still so small. I plan to send her to a good preschool when she's older. I've already submitted a few applications."

"Where did you find this Daisy?" he asked. "Did you do the proper checks into her background to ensure she's trustworthy before you brought her into your home? Did you get several references from other clients?"

Claire sighed. "Yes. I did all that. She came highly recommended, and I haven't had a bit of trouble with her. She's been a godsend over the past few months."

Luca chuckled low and popped a bit of bacon into his mouth. "I know you did all that and more, I'm sure. I was just giving you a hard time, *tesorina*. It is only fair, don't you agree?"

She had given him a lot of grief, she knew that. Claire looked over at Eva as she studiously tried to capture a piece of cereal between her chubby fingers. "I'll do whatever it takes to keep her happy and safe, Luca. Do you blame me?" she asked.

Luca's gaze drifted from the baby back to Claire. There was a fierce fire of protectiveness there as he shook his head. "I do not."

In that moment, it was easy for Claire to believe that Luca would do anything for his young daughter, even after just a few short hours together. He seemed so deeply affected by his child it made her wonder why he hadn't married and started a family of his own by now. He was obviously comfortable with children and took to Eva immediately. Had running the family business really taken up that much of his time that he hadn't found someone to settle down with?

Or was there something he wasn't telling her?

* * *

"What's this?"

Luca looked up from making dinner in time to see Claire standing at the entrance to the kitchen. She was holding up the draft custody agreement his lawyer had given him. He'd left it on the coffee table so they could discuss it. "That's a love note from Edmund. It's the custody proposal we sent to Stuart a few weeks ago. I wasn't entirely sure if you'd read it, so he wanted to make sure we had something to redline while we're here."

A guilty expression wrinkled Claire's nose as she winced. "I didn't read it," she admitted.

Luca wasn't surprised. The woman who sat across from him at his lawyer's office hadn't been interested in his offer. Judging by the expression on her face, not much had changed. He poured dressing onto the bowl of salad for dinner and started gently tossing it. "Would you like to discuss it now?"

Claire eyed the folder and then set it on the kitchen island. "No, not really."

"May I ask why?"

With a sigh, she leaned against the counter. "Because I'm in a good mood. I'm enjoying this trip and I'm not ready to ruin it with our heated arguments. Besides, at this point, my position hasn't changed. You're still a stranger. A stranger who's good with kids, but not one I'm ready to hand over my daughter to."

"*Our* daughter," Luca corrected. She always said "my daughter." Claire seemed to have some kind of mental block where their daughter's paternity was concerned.

Claire ignored him. "My point is that I'm not ready yet, so there's no point in talking about it. I will read it," she added. "So when the time comes, I'll be well informed on your demands."

Demands? Luca wondered whether Claire knew just how her words sounded to him. They were both used to getting their way, but Luca was wise enough to realize they both couldn't win this battle without compromising. "We'll table the discussion, then. Dinner is about done. How about you choose a red wine for tonight?"

Claire went to the wine rack and looked over

the selection. "The chianti or the merlot?" she asked.

Luca pulled the tray of lasagna from the oven and rested it on the stovetop to cool. "The chianti," he said. No question. "We haven't tried that one yet."

Their first week at the beach had gone by in a blur, as vacations often did. Although they'd come here to work out a custody arrangement, they'd both carefully avoided that subject so far. Today, he'd finally gotten out the paperwork to broach the topic, but Claire obviously needed more time. That was fine. Instead of pushing, he took his cues from her, and it had worked. Day by day, Claire had loosened her reins on Eva. He had no doubt that by the end of the trip she would have no problem with him spending time with their daughter alone.

They'd spent a lot of time lounging by the beach and taking walks along the shore. Claire read a couple books and Luca checked in on his work email, although he knew he shouldn't. They cooked amazing meals together, spoiled

Eva together and learned more about each other. It was exactly what Luca had hoped for when they made these arrangements.

Claire had turned out to be a delightful companion. After their first meeting with the lawyers, he had been dreading this trip, but he had been very wrong about her. She was fiercely protective of Eva, but once he got beyond her mother bear instincts, he was pleased to see the more easygoing side of Claire. Once she let her hair down and let the sea air into her lungs, she was just the kind of woman he'd want in his life…if he was ever going to have a woman in his life.

"I can't believe you got Eva to sleep so quickly," Claire said as she carried the bottle of red wine over to the dining-room table.

Luca had been surprised, too, but Eva had had a full day to wear her out. They'd gone down to the beach for a long walk along the bay as they'd done each day. They ate at a seafood shack by the shore where Luca got an amazing fried clam po'boy and Claire got a crab roll. Eva, sadly, got a squeeze pouch of blended chicken, peas and carrots. She took a short nap, then played on the floor for a good while with Claire while Luca assembled their dinner. By the time she had her bath and got put in her pajamas, Eva had heavy eyelids.

"Thanks for letting me put her down tonight," Luca said. It had been the first time he'd gotten to do that since they arrived. He'd stood by her crib, transfixed by his tiny child. He'd even tried out a verse of the lullaby his mother used to sing. Eva was asleep in minutes.

"You're welcome," Claire replied. "I think she likes your singing better than mine, anyway."

"I doubt that. Vacations can be tiring," he said. "She could've slept through anything at that point. To be honest, I'm not sure how much longer I'll last myself. A plate of lasagna and a glass of wine might put me right out."

Claire poured the wine into two glasses at the table beside the place settings she'd already arranged. She grabbed the bowl of salad and walked with Luca to the table to start their feast. "This all smells amazing," she said.

It was Sunday. There was no way that Luca could let the day pass without making an Italian feast that would make his mother proud. "It smells like my mama's kitchen. Garlic, spices, tomato sauce, cheese…Sunday dinner is served."

He cut a large square of lasagna and placed it on Claire's plate, then cut another for himself.

"I am going to gain so much weight," she said as she eyed her meal. "You cook too well and too much, and I can't resist it. It's only been a week, and today my shorts felt a little snug."

"Enjoy yourself," he insisted. "You are so tiny you can afford to put on a few more pounds without worry."

Claire laughed and sipped her wine. "I'm still battling my last few pregnancy pounds, so I assure you that's not the case."

Luca wasn't sure where these mysterious pounds were hidden, but he didn't see them. He actually thought Claire seemed a little thin. He assumed it was the stress of the past year taking its toll on her. "I don't know what you're talk-ing about. You look amazing to me. My mother would insist you're too skinny and force food on you if I were to bring you home to her."

He flinched inwardly as the words slipped from his mouth. Claire seemed to stiffen in her chair beside him, and he knew it felt strange for her to think of him that way, as well. He'd never considered what it would be like for Claire to meet the rest of his family. And really, bringing Claire to the house wasn't the same as bringing home a girlfriend. It was far more complicated.

Claire finally relaxed when he didn't push the subject and just shook her head. "I can't even imagine," she said. "How did your family take the news about Eva?"

"I haven't told them yet," Luca admitted.

"Why is that?"

Luca sighed, exhausted by the mere idea of telling his family, much less doing it. "Well, as I told you before, I have a big family. I also have a loud, pushy, smothering family. I think my mother has very nearly given up on me ever having children. Finding out about Eva would be earth-shattering. They would swarm on us like bees on a honeycomb. I wanted us to have a little space first. Getting away from Manhattan was a part of that. They'll find out soon enough."

As far as Luca was concerned, they were already on borrowed time. He'd been very careful, but he awaited a leak any day now. Every time his phone buzzed at his hip, he expected to see his mother's number on the screen.

"Where do they think you are now? I mean, you had to get someone to run the company while you're gone all these weeks, right?"

"I told my brothers that I was taking a beautiful woman away on a vacation. They agreed to handle things and not tell anyone. Probably because they're as desperate as Mama to see me find a woman."

"Do you feel bad about lying to them?"

Luca's brows drew together in confusion. "No. I'm not lying."

"But you said—"

"I said I was taking a beautiful woman on a

vacation." Luca looked at her across the table. "That's absolutely true."

That rose blush spread across Claire's cheeks again, distracting him from his plate. "Quit it. You don't have to butter me up."

Luca set his fork down. Claire might be a fierce competitor in their lawyers' offices, but when it came to romance, she seemed almost broken by the idea of it. "I'm not flattering you, *tesorina*. I'm serious. Are you not aware of how attractive you are?"

Her mouth fell open, a flustered conglomeration of nonsense words coming out of her as she tried to gather her thoughts. "I mean, I think I'm pretty enough. I'm no supermodel or polished Upper East Side housewife."

"Fake," he said. "All of that is fake, crafted by makeup artists, plastic surgeons and photo-altering software. I will take a real, soft, naturally beautiful woman over one of those fantasies any day."

"I think you're in the minority, Luca."

Luca couldn't stand the uncomfortable expression on Claire's face. Was this just Jeff's doing, or had every man in her life treated her poorly? "Did your husband never tell you how beautiful you were?"

Claire looked down and anxiously moved her food around on her plate for a moment. "Not really. I mean, he chose me, so he must've thought I was pretty, but he wasn't the type to lay on praise. Especially near the end."

Luca sat back in his chair for a minute and tried to absorb everything she'd just told him. He would never have a wife of his own, but he knew if he did he would cherish her. "I'm sorry," he said at last.

Claire's eyes widened with surprise. "You're sorry for what?" she asked.

"I'm sorry that your husband didn't treat you the way he should have." Just hearing her talk about Jeff had made his blood boil. Not only had he been reckless with his marriage, he'd been reckless with his life when he had a child on the way. Then to find out that he'd never given his wife the love and praise she deserved even in the early years of their relationship… It was inexcusable in his eyes.

"We were having trouble," Claire argued. "I was so wrapped up in the idea of having a baby that I forgot about having a marriage. I think he was lonely."

"That is no excuse," Luca said, leaning in to her and covering her hand with his. "It is natural for a woman to want a child. When there are difficulties, her husband should be more attentive and supportive than ever. To stray from your bed because he felt like he wasn't getting enough attention is absurd. I was always raised to believe that a woman is meant to be treasured. She is a gift, an angel sent into your life from the heavens. To treat her as anything less is an abomination."

Claire watched him speak with a mix of disbelief and wonder in her gray eyes. She leaned into him, her lips parting. They were soft, plump lips that had gone too long without kisses. That was a tragedy in Luca's eyes. A few kind words and she was melting like butter. She deserved better. Unfortunately, Luca was not the man to give it to her. He sat back and pulled his hand away.

She snapped out of her trance and moved her hand down into her lap. "Do you really believe all that?" she asked.

"I do. My parents have been married for over thirty years keeping that philosophy in mind."

"May I ask why you haven't married, then? I'm sure there are plenty of women out there who would love you to treat them like a precious gift."

Luca tried not to stiffen at her question. He had done his fair share of prying into her personal life; it shouldn't be out of bounds for her to do the same. But there were land mines in this field he didn't want to hit. Not tonight and not ever. Instead, he shrugged and relied on the story he had told again and again over the years.

"Since the day I was born, I was groomed to take over the family business. Moretti's has always had the oldest son running the company. I went from high school to college to grad school to the boardroom. Once my father retired, I had this huge weight on my shoulders to keep the company running and profitable, or I would be letting everyone down. That hasn't really left me much time for anything else. Not just relationships, either. I never travel. I have almost no hobbies or interests outside of work. I have my business. That's it."

What Luca left out was that it was all by design. His father had managed to run the company while having time for his wife and children, so he knew it could be done, but keeping busy was the only way Luca could get through the lonely times. Claire wouldn't understand that, though, because she didn't realize he was damaged. She only saw the successful, confident businessman he portrayed to the world.

"You've never been in love before?"

Luca considered his answer before speaking. "No," he lied. "I got close, but I was wrong."

"That's kind of sad," Claire said. "For all your money and success, all you have to show for it is money and success. You don't even get to enjoy it with someone. When was the last time you took a vacation?"

"I'm on a vacation right now," Luca argued.

"No. Before this one."

Luca thought back, but he knew there wasn't really an answer. "I've never taken a vacation as an adult. Not a real one, at least. Occasionally my family gathers for a long weekend in the Hamptons during the summer."

"It sounds like you're going to be an old, lonely bachelor before too long. What will your family do if you don't have an oldest son to take over after you?"

That was a question that had plagued Luca since the day of his diagnosis. In reality, there were plenty of people in the family who could take the reins. His younger brother Marcello had a son who could easily be the next CEO. But now he had a new possibility. "Well, this isn't the fifties anymore. It isn't written anywhere that it has to be a son. I may not marry or have any more children, but through a twist of fate, I do have Eva in my life. It's always a possibility that she could take over for me."

"If she wants to," Claire countered. "It's nice to have a family legacy, but I don't want her pressured into a life and a career she doesn't want."

"Of course." Luca didn't want that for his daughter, either. He hadn't been pressured into taking the company over, thankfully. It was something he'd always dreamed of doing. His family was important to him and carrying that legacy on was an honor. He'd once hoped that he could pass it along to his child, too, but that was a fantasy he'd given up years ago. "We have the next three weeks to worry about before we need be concerned with Eva's career path."

Claire nodded and turned back to her food. Luca watched her eat for a moment, sipping his wine thoughtfully. At this angle, he could see the faint gray circles under her eyes and the defeated slope of her shoulders. The stress wasn't just wearing her thin. It was eating away at her.

He recognized the look from the days his mother sat at his bedside at the hospital, worrying over him. He hadn't been in any condition to help his mother, but he could help Claire, if she'd let him. Being a single mother had to be incredibly difficult, even with resources at her disposal. She needed this vacation more than even he knew.

They had come here to get to know each other and hash out a custody arrangement, but now he had a different goal: to find a way to make Claire happy again.

Five

Claire couldn't sleep that night. Her head was spinning with everything Luca had said to her at dinner. She wasn't sure if he was telling the truth or if he had the ability to charm a woman by knowing exactly what she needed to hear. They'd spent only a week together. Was she that easy to read? Either way, it was working. A combination of gentle words and strong wine had weakened her defenses. By the time they'd finished eating and cleaned up the kitchen, she would've agreed to anything he suggested. Even the kind of things she knew were a bad idea.

Like touching him. All through dinner she wanted to run her fingers though the dark waves of his hair. She wanted to brush the pad of her thumb over his bottom lip as he spoke the words she'd longed for a man to say to her her whole life. What would he do if she reached out to him? Would he pull her into his arms or push her away? Would he call her *tesorina*? She had no idea what it meant, but whenever he said it she felt her knees soften beneath her.

Now there was a restlessness inside her, keeping sleep at bay. An ache deep in her belly. She didn't know if it was heartburn from the spicy tomato sauce or her long-dormant desire coming back to life, but neither was welcome.

She'd come here to get to know her baby's father, but not in the biblical sense. After her disastrous relationship with Jeff, she'd resigned herself to not falling in love again. It was too hard on her heart, and she didn't think she could take that risk a second time. If she did, she needed a man who was first and foremost honest, and she couldn't trust a word out of Luca's mouth right now. They were on opposite sides of this custody battle. But between the beautiful beach views, the amazing meals and the stimulating conversation, it was easy to let that slip her mind. That would be a dangerous mistake, as she was pretty certain Luca wouldn't do the same.

Frustrated, she flung back the blankets and headed out into the living room. Tonight, she'd been warm from the wine, so she'd opted for a thin, baby-doll nightgown with spaghetti straps. It was short and nearly see-through, but she couldn't bear to put on her flannel pants and top when she went to bed.

Fortunately the house was dark and quiet when she stepped into the hallway, so her attire wouldn't matter. Claire wasn't entirely sure what she was after, but she ended up in the kitchen. She didn't bother turning on the lights. Doing that would ensure she'd never sleep.

Instead, the moonlight through the windows illuminated what she needed to see. Deciding on a cup of tea, she found some in the cupboard and put a mug of water in the microwave to heat. She opened the refrigerator door, looking around for something of interest, but nothing caught her eye. When the water was warmed, she shut the refrigerator and pulled the mug out of the microwave. She let the tea bag steep, then added some honey to sweeten it.

It took a moment for her eyes to adjust to the darkness again, but when they did, she turned and noticed a large, dark figure standing at the edge of the kitchen.

A jolt of panic rushed through her as the shape came closer, until she recognized Luca's gait. Finally, the moonlight from the window lit him, and her heartbeat started to return to normal. Well, at least until she realized he was wearing nothing but a pair of boxer shorts.

The silver light highlighted the curves of his muscular arms and cut of his chest. The sprinkle of dark hair across his chest narrowed and ran down his belly. Her eyes followed the trail along his hard abs, and she felt the heartburn start to rage more intensely inside her.

Okay, it wasn't heartburn, she admitted to herself. It was desire. She'd almost forgotten what that felt like.

When her gaze drifted back up to Luca's face, there was a faint curl of a smile on his lips. Could he tell she was checking him out?

"Are you okay?" he asked.

"Yes. I just couldn't sleep."

"Me, neither." His gaze drifted over her thin nightie with appreciation in his eyes. His jaw clenched tightly, making her wonder if they were both suffering from the same cause of insomnia.

"Would you like some tea?" she asked, distracting herself. "I just made myself some chamomile with honey."

"No, thank you."

As he continued to stand there, Claire felt herself at a loss. She could sense the tension in the air between them. It was electric, yet neither of them seemed willing to do anything about it. Probably because they both knew it was a bad idea. And yet...

Claire needed to go back to her room, drink

her tea and go to sleep. That was the *only* thing she needed to do. She just had to get past Luca's hulking figure blocking the path between the fridge and the kitchen island. "Well, good night then," she said. Dropping her gaze to the mug in her hands, she pressed forward, expecting Luca to move out of the way.

But he didn't.

Instead, she felt his hand catch her waist. The heat of his skin burned through the thin fabric of her gown, nearly branding her with his touch. "Claire?"

She stopped cold, her breath catching in her throat. Using just one word, he'd asked a hundred different questions at once. She turned her head to look up at him. He was looking down at her, with his own ragged breaths making his chest rise and fall as though he'd been running. He swallowed hard, the muscles in his throat contracting. She watched his tongue snake over his bottom lip. All the while, his intense eyes were devouring her.

Claire knew in that moment that whatever

question he was asking, the answer was yes. Setting down the mug of tea, she turned to him. "Yes."

Luca didn't hesitate. He scooped her up into his arms and pulled her hard against his chest. His mouth met hers with the ferocity of a man dying of thirst and she was his glass of water. He drank her in and Claire was powerless to stop it. She didn't want to. It had been too long since she'd been desired. Wanted. Jeff had never once in their years of marriage kissed her with as much passion as Luca did in this moment. She didn't want to let that go.

Claire wrapped her arms around his neck and arched her back to press her hips into him. She felt the evidence of his desire there, insistently nudging against her. He groaned her name against her mouth when they made contact, then spun her around until her back was touching the cold stainless steel of the refrigerator. The chill did little to dampen the heat building inside her. With every stroke of his tongue and graze of his hand along her body, he stoked the flames that she'd once thought had died out for good.

When she felt his hand slip beneath her night-gown and his fingers brush the lacy trim of her panties, she felt the slightest hesitation. Like a lightning bolt, it startled her out of the hormone-driven haze she'd fallen into. Things had moved fast. Too fast. Was she really ready to have sex in the kitchen with a man she barely knew? The man who was trying to take Eva from her?

Before she could answer, the sharp, angry wail of her daughter interrupted her thoughts. It wasn't Eva's usual cry for hunger or a wet diaper. Something was wrong.

Luca stilled and pulled away, his lips a fraction of an inch from hers. He was breathing hard, likely cursing his bad luck and hoping that Eva would fall back asleep. That wasn't going to happen.

Claire pushed against Luca's chest and he took a step back. "I'm sorry, I have to go check on the baby." She fled the kitchen as quickly as she could, both out of concern and awkwardness.

That situation had quickly gotten out of control, and thankfully Eva woke at just the right time to keep things from going too far.

Entering the bedroom, she turned on the lamp and scooped her red faced and teary daughter from her crib. "What's the matter, baby?" she asked, but the second Claire's cheek touched Eva's, she knew what was wrong.

Eva was burning up with fever.

Claire started frantically searching through her diaper bag for the baby thermometer. Her desire-addled thoughts were scrambled by the sharp cries in her ear. "Shhh, you're okay," she soothed, but Eva could not be comforted. Poor, sick baby.

"Is she okay?"

Claire turned to find Luca in her doorway. "She has a fever." She finally located the thermometer and placed it inside the infant's ear. "One hundred and three."

That seemed high. She felt the panic start to well up inside her. She hadn't brought her baby book. She was hours away from Eva's pediatrician. She knew that the seriousness varied by age and temperature, but she didn't recall what the cutoff was for calling the doctor. The louder Eva cried, the harder it was for her to try to focus.

"Here," Luca said, gently taking Eva from her arms.

"What do you think you're doing?" Claire asked.

"I'm taking care of our sick child." Ignoring her irritable tone, Luca immediately started unsnapping Eva's onesie. He seemed unfazed by the sharp screams of his daughter, so in control when Claire felt anything but. "I'm going to put her in a cool bath to make her more comfortable. Do you have any medication to bring down her fever?"

She nodded. "It's in the diaper bag. I'll dig it out."

Luca disappeared into the master bathroom and Claire quickly dug around in the bag until she found the medicine. By the time she joined Luca in the bathroom, Eva had started to quiet down. She was lying in her bath chair in a shallow pool of water while Luca rubbed a damp sponge over her skin. The lukewarm water and lavender scented bubbles seemed to soothe her. After a few minutes, the tears were dried, and while she still seemed a little cranky and uncomfortable, they'd made good progress.

At last, Luca lifted Eva up into her yellow bath towel with the ducky hood and bundled her up. He squeezed the dropper of medicine into Eva's mouth and handed the bottle back to Claire. "While I get her dried off, can you make her a bottle with cool water in it? She might be a little dehydrated from the fever, and it will make her more comfortable."

Claire nodded and wandered off toward the kitchen, feeling oddly useless as Luca took charge. She wasn't even entirely sure what had just happened, aside from the fact that in a crucial moment she'd choked and given Luca the window of opportunity he'd been waiting for. When she reached the kitchen, she eyed her abandoned mug of tea and the smudged refrigerator and shook her head. Apparently tonight was a night of missteps.

At the same time, she was happy to have someone here with her. This was Eva's first real fever, and although she thought she was prepared for it, she'd been completely off her game coming fresh from Luca's kisses. She supposed that was the benefit of having two parents, to split the responsibility and pick up the slack for the other. She didn't know what that was like.

As she filled a small bottle with filtered water, she felt the unexpected prickle of tears in her eyes. This was just one more moment to remind her what she'd lost with Jeff's recklessness. Her dreams of having a family had been shattered, creating a new reality that was so much harder than she ever imagined. He'd left her to raise a child alone all so he could get a hand job on a winding road.

"Claire?"

Claire quickly batted her tears away and sniffed. She tightened the bottle's cap and turned to face him. "It's ready. How is she doing?"

Luca watched her with concern as he took the bottle. "I think she'll be okay. I'm not so sure about you, though."

"Me?" She must not have done as good a job of hiding her emotions as she thought.

"Eva's going to be fine, you know. There's nothing to be worried about."

Claire nodded in agreement. "I know."

"Okay, so what is bothering you then?"

That was a loaded question. "Something. Everything. Don't worry about me, Luca, really. Lately, I seem to have too many hot buttons for life to push."

Luca adjusted Eva in his arms and gave her the bottle. "Is it the kiss? Did I press you too quickly?"

"No," she admitted. "The kiss was…lovely. Probably not the best idea for us, but I don't regret it."

"Then did I overstep with Eva tonight? I'm sorry if that's it, but you seemed a bit overwhelmed and I wanted to help. My youngest sister had a lot of ear infections when she was little and was prone to fevers. I've spent more than a few nights up with my mother bathing fussy babies."

That explained a lot. Despite being a mother, Claire was learning as she went. As an only child, she didn't have any experience caring for children. Her every move was a mix between her research and maternal instincts. "No, that's not it, either. Thank you for all your help with her. You're right, I was feeling a little frazzled in the moment and was glad to have someone step in. I shouldn't need help, but it's nice to have it every now and then."

Luca placed a comforting hand on Claire's shoulder. The warmth of him against her bare skin reminded her of his earlier touches, sending a shiver running down her spine. It wasn't just about temperatures, though. The simple feel of his large, strong hands on her body was enough for her to want to pick up where they'd left off a few minutes ago.

Suddenly, she was aware of how close Luca was and how good he smelled. It had been a long time since she'd been touched by a man, even in comfort. For some reason, that combination along with Luca's radiating masculinity was more than she could take. Of course she'd given into it. Any woman in her position would have. He told her she was beautiful. They had a child together. He kissed her as if there was nothing more in the world he could ever desire. But once the spell of their kiss faded away, she knew that nothing more could come of it.

There was a wall up when it came to Luca. She could tell the moment their discussions went off into uncomfortable territory for him. Even the most harmless questions about his high-school prom seemed to set a glaze over his eyes. The answers that followed felt hollow and inauthentic. Not necessarily that he was lying, but that his response was practiced. Claire had her fair share of practiced speeches with Jeff as he successfully hid his infidelity. She wasn't about to make that mistake twice, even with a man who was ten times more thoughtful and charming than Jeff ever was.

"You're a mother, *tesorina*, not a superhero. It's okay to accept help."

"Thank you." Claire knew that, at least in theory. Putting it into practice was harder. Aside from Daisy, she didn't really have anyone to lean on for help. Despite the messy circumstances, perhaps having Luca in Eva's life wouldn't be so bad. There would be someone else she could call when she needed help, and when Eva stayed with her father, Claire would get the occasional break to recharge and relax. She didn't realize just how much she needed that until this moment. She wasn't quite ready to just give in on the custody agreement yet, but she was starting to see the silver lining of the situation.

"I'll stay up with her for a while if you want to go back to bed."

Claire immediately felt anxious about his offer. It was one thing to let him help and another entirely to let him take over. She hated questioning his every motivation, but she couldn't be naive. What could he tell the judge then? That when Eva was sick, he was the one who had to care for her? No, thanks. "That won't be necessary," she said, reaching to take Eva from his arms. "I was having trouble sleeping anyway. I'm going to stay up until she starts feeling better."

Luca didn't immediately release Eva. He watched Claire suspiciously, and she fought to swallow the onset of an unexpected yawn. "I think the sandman is ready for you now. My time will come later. We'll be fine, I promise. Go back to bed. I'll wake you up if something happens. Otherwise, I'll rock her until she falls back to sleep and put her in her crib."

Claire was resistant, but she could tell by the firm, yet gentle expression on Luca's face that he would insist. Perhaps he was just being nice and not looking for ammunition to use against her in court. Her eyelids were getting too heavy for her to argue any longer. "Okay, thank you. I'll leave the door open to the bedroom."

"Good night," he said with Eva snuggled into his arms.

She could tell that Eva would probably be asleep before she was. Not much to worry about, then. She reluctantly returned to her bedroom and burrowed beneath the down comforter. With the late night emotional highs, quickly came the lows. Before she knew it, she crashed.

The last thought as she drifted to sleep was how Luca's lips had felt as they pressed against hers. And she wondered—would she ever feel that again?

It seemed as though she'd just closed her eyes when she opened them to daylight streaming through the window. Claire sat up in bed, noticing the bedroom door was still open and the crib remained empty. If Eva hadn't fallen asleep, why hadn't Luca woken her up?

Climbing from bed, she pulled on her robe and returned to the living room. She expected to find them milling around the kitchen or out on the deck, but it seemed as though things hadn't gone as Luca planned. There on the couch under a chenille blanket, she found Luca and Eva. Both were asleep, with Eva curled into a little ball on his chest. Claire stood there for a moment, watching the two of them together. It was precious. They both made the same little grumpy faces while they dreamed, their brows drawn together and their lips pouty in sleepy consternation. She wanted to capture the memory of them together like this and never forget it.

"Good morning."

Claire was startled to notice Luca's eyes had opened, and he was watching her as closely as she was watching him. "Morning. You two look pretty cozy."

Luca looked down at the infant drooling on his bare chest. "I guess so. We must've conked out pretty quickly after you went to bed. I don't think I've moved an inch the whole night." He sat up slowly as to not disturb the baby, groaning softly as he stretched his stiff limbs. "What time is it?"

"A little after nine."

"Wow." Luca ran one hand through the messy waves of his hair and shook his head. "I haven't slept that late in years."

Claire approached him and held out her arms

to relieve him of Eva for a while. "I'll take Eva. Why don't you take a shower to loosen up, and I'll make us all some breakfast."

Luca stood and handed off the sleeping infant. "Please make coffee. Strong, black coffee."

"I can do that."

He started toward the staircase, but before he could reach it, Claire said, "Luca?" He stopped and turned. "I wanted to say thank you."

"For what?" he asked.

"For last night."

He gave her a guilty smirk in response. "Which part? The part where I lost control and almost took you against the refrigerator? Or the part where I pushed you aside to take care of Eva when I could tell you didn't want me to?"

That was a good question. The words had leaped from her lips before she'd really thought them through. "Both, maybe. The combination of those two things gave me a little taste of what it's like to have someone in my life again. To help me, to hold me. It was nice."

"I know what you mean," he said. "I think you

and I have both gotten too used to being alone. My mother is always reminding me that's not how people are supposed to live. I'm starting to think she's right."

"I may not know you that well, but from what I've seen you're a good man, Luca. The woman you let into your life would be very lucky."

A sadness Claire didn't understand washed over Luca's face. Why would a compliment like that steal the light from his eyes so quickly when her angry insults of the past didn't seem to make the slightest dent in his armor?

"Thank you," he said, but she got the feeling he didn't believe it, just as she didn't believe it when he told her she was beautiful. They both seemed to have a lot of doubts when it came to their self-worth and value to the opposite sex. Claire knew why she felt that way, but Luca? He was an attractive, thoughtful and wealthy businessman with a way of complimenting a woman so her knees turned to butter. She wasn't sure why he wasn't fighting women off with a stick. He wasn't the kind of man she needed in her life, but he would be a great choice for any other woman.

Claire wanted him to know that she really meant what she'd said, that it wasn't just some flattery. "I wish I'd found a man more like you when I was younger and looking for someone to start my life with. If I had, perhaps I wouldn't be a widow wondering how her life went off track."

The sadness faded away and Luca's jaw tightened along with his grip on the banister. He looked up at her with eyes that reflected a confusing combination of regret and irritation. "If I were you, I wouldn't waste my wishes on a man like me," he said, and headed downstairs.

Six

Luca sat in a beach chair quietly scowling. Claire was with Eva as they carefully splashed in the waves. The baby was wearing a rainbow-striped swimsuit with ruffles on her bottom, although most of her was held out of the water by her mother. Eva would squeal every time the cold water rushed over her feet, then giggle as if it was the greatest thing she'd ever experienced. If Claire let go of her hands, Eva would grab fistfuls of wet sand and mush them between her fingers.

It should've been a happy and amusing sight

for Luca. He should be out there in the freezing water with his daughter. Instead, he was sitting at a distance, practically pouting beneath his ball cap and sunglasses. He had no reason to pout, really. He'd succeeded in pushing Claire away. That was what he'd wanted to do, or at least what he felt he had to do when she got that moony look in her eyes. He might have slipped up the other night and let himself get carried away physically, but that didn't change the fact that he was not the man for Claire. He wasn't a romantic savior there to sweep in and rescue her from her loneliness. It was better that she learn that now rather than later.

And yet the past few days had been miserable. At first, Claire had been focused on Eva and caring for her as she got over her illness. When the baby was well, she continued to keep her distance. She wasn't rude, but she wasn't as open and chatty as she had been before.

He should've been content that she got the message. Instead, Luca was surprised to find himself missing their talks. He'd also found himself lying in bed at night thinking about the kiss they'd shared in the kitchen. Lord help him, he couldn't stop himself. Once he got a taste of her, it was as if something had been unleashed deep inside him. Every touch, every soft sound she made, urged him on. If Eva hadn't woken up with that fever, he wasn't sure what would've happened.

He could tell that Claire was relieved by the interruption. They'd been caught up in the moment. Time and perspective would prove it wasn't the best idea in their situation. It didn't change how much he wanted her, though. The next morning, when she seemed more open to the idea than he expected, he wasn't sure what to do. Claire was not a casual romance type of woman, that was obvious. He'd done a better job of charming her than he'd intended to, and suddenly he found himself in a position he hadn't expected.

So he pushed back. It was the best thing to do, really. Claire deserved a relationship with a man who could give her everything she wanted, including love and another child. That wasn't going to be Luca, no matter how badly he ached for her. It was better to put a stop to all this before it went too far.

Looking back out at the sea, Luca couldn't help but admire Claire's figure on display. Despite her claims of excess baby weight, she looked great in her shorts and bikini top. Her skin was golden from their time at the beach, and the blond in her hair seemed to be picking up some lighter streaks from the sun. Her curves were highlighted by the halter cut of the bikini, giving him a tantalizing glimpse of her full breasts.

There was nothing not to like about Claire. That was the problem. It was too easy to like her. Too easy to find a reason to touch her. His blood would sing in his veins whenever he caught a whiff of her scent. There was a restlessness in every muscle when he lay alone thinking about her upstairs in the dark. It was as if his body knew they had a child together and was ready to start on another one as soon as possible.

And if Luca could provide that for her, he might be in the water instead of sulking in his chair. But he couldn't. Luca would rather live his life a bachelor than a disappointment to the woman he loved. His only alternative would be to find a woman who couldn't have children of her own. They didn't exactly walk around advertising that fact, however.

Looking back at the water, he noticed Claire and Eva had moved to drier sand to play with the plastic bucket and shovel they'd carried to the beach with them. Looking at the dark curls of his daughter, all he could do was shake his head. What a bizarre twist of fate that would give him a child. It was like a perfectly imperfect storm that brought two people together to have a child neither of them expected to have.

Wait a minute…Luca sat up taller in his chair. Claire may very well be that woman. She hadn't spoken extensively about her fertility issues, but she had to have some or she wouldn't have been at the clinic. He'd avoided the subject, as well.

He didn't like people knowing he had cancer, much less the kind he'd had.

Luca wasn't the type to really believe in fate, but life certainly seemed to be convincing him otherwise. What if Claire was the chance he'd never let himself believe in? If he let their attraction evolve into a relationship, this could be his second chance. It would work out perfectly. They already had a child together. If they were to marry, it would tidy up the whole custody situation. He'd get the full-time family he wanted, and Claire wouldn't have to be away from Eva when it was his weekend.

Claire approached his chair with a sand-covered baby in her arms. "I'm going to hose this little monkey off and put her down for a nap."

"Okay. I'll pack up and be back at the house in a few minutes."

He watched Claire disappear, their dating scenario playing out in his mind. Wooing her was the perfect solution. It had been dropped in his lap, really. They'd both benefit from the scenario. Claire would get a full-time father for Eva and a man to treat her the way she deserved to be treated. Luca would get the family he never thought he'd have, and he'd get his mother off his back once and for all. It would be nice to have someone to come home to, to talk to. His apartment was becoming unbearably empty.

Never mind the fact that he'd finally get to touch her. Seducing Claire would be the best part of this plan. No holding back, no excuses, no interruptions. He'd get to run his hands along those long legs and cup her breasts in his needy palms. Luca was hardly celibate, but thinking about Claire made him as eager as a virgin. And as nervous.

He'd only attempted to be in a relationship once before, and it hadn't ended well. Even if he'd wanted to try again, he'd hardly had the time. The best he could manage was a few dates with a woman before things got in the way and she'd break it off. Aside from Jessica, he'd never even dated a woman long enough to consider her his girlfriend, much less look ahead to her being his wife. Could he do it now for his daughter's sake?

Reluctantly, Luca got up from his chair and started gathering their things in a bag. With every toy he stuffed inside, the more certain he became that the answer was yes. He'd do anything for that little girl. She was the child he never expected, and he wanted her to have a real family. Despite what Claire thought, he didn't want Eva shuttled back and forth between households, caught up in visitation agreements and who gets which holidays. That meant taking a chance on having that real family with Claire.

But would Claire want anything to do with him? He'd pretty much told her he wasn't a candidate for any of her romantic notions. She'd had an unhappy marriage and wouldn't settle for the same this time. She'd want love and passion and everything that went with it. Luca would happily give her the passion and attention she needed. Love was another matter. He'd already made the mistake of giving that too freely once, and it had blown up in his face. That could happen with Claire, too, if he wasn't careful.

He slung the bag over his shoulder and started

back up the sandy path through the dunes. He knew that if Claire found out what was wrong with him, she would feel betrayed, bringing up all the emotions of her first husband's infidelity. To protect himself from the possibility of being hit with emotional shrapnel, he'd have to keep his emotions soundly out of the equation.

That meant she couldn't know the truth. Not about his cancer and not about how he really felt. He'd have to make sure he did everything right so she'd never question his love for her. It wouldn't be hard to treat her better than Jeff had. Just a kind word was enough to make her melt. She deserved better than he'd treated her. Luca might not let himself love Claire, but he'd certainly do everything in his power to make her feel loved.

By the time he reached the house, Luca knew exactly how he would start his bid for Claire's affections. To do it right, he knew he'd have to take the ultimate risk—to call his sister in Newport.

* * *

There was something different about Luca. Claire had tried to give him his space the past few days after their unexpected encounter. He'd given her confusing signals, so she decided that perhaps that kiss was the result of exhaustion and bad judgment. That was probably for the best, anyway, if this was how he was going to react to something like that. He'd been quiet and withdrawn, almost moody.

But since they'd come back from the beach, his mood had greatly improved. When she was done bathing Eva and put her down for her nap, she'd come out of the master bedroom to find him humming to himself and cooking up something tasty in the kitchen. The dark cloud that had hovered over him the past few days had disappeared, and she wasn't sure whether she should be happy about it. It was easier to ignore Luca's charms when he was distant and scowling. The smiling, happy Luca wore away her resistance too easily.

"I have a surprise," he announced when he noticed her in the living room.

Claire wasn't that good with surprises. More times than not it wasn't a good thing. "What?"

"My baby sister, Mia, is coming to the house tonight."

Claire couldn't help the frown that instantly furrowed her brow. That was not at all what she'd expected him to say. Luca had made a point of telling her that he'd kept Eva and the whole situation from his family, and yet he seemed awfully chipper for a man who hadn't had things go his way. "Why? Did she find out about Eva?"

"Yes," he admitted, "but only because I told her. I actually invited her to stay with us for a few days. Mia lives not far from here in Newport."

She was listening, but she couldn't quite figure out what was going on. Eva was a huge secret, then suddenly he was rolling out the red carpet for his family? "I'm confused," she said. "Why did you tell her? Does your whole family know the truth now?"

"If my whole family knows the truth, I'm going to skin Mia, so no, they don't all know. I just told her and swore her to secrecy."

"Again," Claire pressed. "Why?" Was he so uncomfortable being alone with her now that he took the risk of inviting his sister here?

"So we could have a babysitter," Luca said with a smile. "I'm taking you out tomorrow. I've got a whole day planned. Mia is going to stay here with Eva so you can relax and enjoy yourself."

Taking her out? "I appreciate the gesture, Luca, but I'm not sure about this. I don't even know your sister. I don't know how comfortable I'm going to be leaving Eva with her."

"Mia is great with kids, I promise. Not only is she an elementary school teacher, she's watched all of my nieces and nephews a hundred times. She will be fine with Eva while we're gone."

It all seemed sensible, and yet Claire felt her hackles go up with his presumptuous tone. He seemed to think Eva was an asset of his corporation, not a child she had any say in. "That's all well and good, Luca, but you didn't even ask me before making that decision. This is the kind of stuff that worries me about our arrangements. I don't mind letting you in on some of the parenting decisions, but I'm not about to get pushed out of them entirely."

Luca seemed dumbfounded by her irritation. Could he really not see what he was doing while he was doing it?

"Fair enough," he said after a moment's consideration. "I'll leave the final decision up to you. When you meet Mia, you can decide if you trust her to watch Eva. If so, I'll take you out. If not, my sister will just be visiting for a few days."

Claire sighed with relief. All she wanted was a voice in the process, even if she already knew that in the end she'd let his sister watch Eva so they could go out. Whatever was going on with Luca had inspired all of this, and despite what he'd just agreed to, he wasn't likely to change his mind easily. He wanted to take her out, so she would let him. It might actually be nice. It had been a long time since she'd had an evening out for a little grown-up time. She worked so much that she felt guilty leaving Eva with a sitter after spending all day with Daisy.

"When will she be here?" she asked instead.

Luca glanced down at his watch. "Less than an hour. She texted me when she got on the ferry. She'll definitely be here in time to eat, so I thought I'd make her favorite chicken tetrazzini. Does that sound okay to you?"

Claire chuckled and walked past him to the refrigerator to get a drink. "Any meal I don't have to cook is great by me. It certainly doesn't hurt that you're an excellent cook."

"I'm a passable cook," Luca clarified. "My sister is an amazing cook. You'll see."

"Does your sister know you just invited her up here to watch children and cook?"

Luca laughed. "When my family gets together, that's what we do. Lots of food, laughter, playful bickering and kids. You keep an eye on whichever one is closest. It won't faze her in the slightest, but yes, I did tell her why I wanted her to come up. She's excited to meet you and Eva."

Claire wished she was as excited to meet his sister. She suddenly felt anxious about the whole thing for an entirely different reason. What would his family think of her? Would they hate her for fighting Luca for custody? Would they read something into the two of them being here together, alone? Her stomach started to ache with worry. She was a fairly quiet and reserved woman who often came off to strangers as aloof or stuck-up. What if they didn't like her?

"Are you okay?" Luca asked. "You don't look very excited about Mia coming."

"I'm fine. I'm just a little nervous about meeting some of your family, is all. I'm not really the loud, laughter type."

Luca turned away from his sautéing chicken to take Claire's hands. He pulled them to his chest and held them there. Claire's breath caught in her throat. She could feel his heart pounding in his rib cage almost in time with her own. His dark gaze focused on her. This close, she could see the gold and caramel colored flecks in his hazel eyes. Looking into them, she started to relax. He could have such a soothing effect on her one moment, then with a simple wicked smile, he could heat her cheeks and make her think thoughts she hadn't entertained in a very long time.

"You're going to be fine," he insisted. "Mia will love you, and when you meet the rest of my family, they'll love you, too. They're used to intimidating new people, so if you're quiet, they'll think it's them, not you. Besides, just meeting Mia without everyone else will be a nice ice-breaker."

"Are you not worried about the rest of your family finding out what's going on?" Claire didn't care if his family found out the truth, but she knew it concerned him. She didn't know what it was like to have a large, overbearing family, so she didn't understand his issues with them. This did seem out of character for him, though. What had changed his mind? That was a big change just for the opportunity to go out to dinner.

Or was it more than that?

"There's always that risk," Luca said. "But things will be fine. I wouldn't have called Mia if I didn't think I could trust her. Carla, on the other hand, would blab to everyone. And even if they did find out, it will be okay. I think you and I are getting along pretty well and can probably work out a custody arrangement we're both comfortable with. Eva seems to have taken to me. Besides, it's not like we're engaged or something."

Claire was following along until he brought up that last point. It was true, but for some reason it bothered her to hear him say it so dismissively. It must be because it felt like something. It felt like more than it was because of their daughter and the strange circumstances. In truth, all they'd shared was a kiss. They hadn't even gone out on a date. Whatever this beach house arrangement was, it wasn't a date.

Pulling away so he wouldn't see the touch of disappointment in her eyes, she started to walk from the kitchen. "I'm going to spiffy up for company."

"Okay," she heard Luca say, but she didn't turn around.

In her suite, she changed from her yoga pants into a sundress, then sat at her vanity staring at herself in the mirror. She fussed with her hair for a while, not happy, but finally settling on putting it up in a bun. She applied a little lip gloss and mascara. They might be on a lazy beach vacation, but she didn't want to look like it when she met his sister. If Mia did report back to the family, Claire didn't want them to think she was a slacker.

As she was finishing up, she heard voices in the other room and knew that Mia must have arrived. The noise finally woke Eva from her nap, so Claire changed her and put her in a cute pink-and-yellow dress to meet her aunt.

By the time they went into the living room, Luca and a pretty young woman were seated on the couch drinking wine. Luca immediately stood up and gestured toward his sister. "Claire, this is my sister Mia. Mia, this is Claire and my daughter, Eva."

Mia looked like a petite version of Luca, with long, curly brown hair, rich, olive skin and wide, dark eyes. It made Claire wonder if that was what Eva might look like when she grew up. She didn't have long to ponder, though. Mia launched up from the couch and embraced Claire before she could prepare herself.

"Oh my goodness," she declared as she pulled away and examined Claire. "She's beautiful, Luca! Why didn't you tell me how pretty she was?"

"Because I didn't want you scheming," Luca said with a smile.

"I would never," Mia argued with an equally wicked grin. She winked at Claire, then turned her attention to the baby. "And aren't you the most precious little girl I've ever laid my eyes on!"

The next thing Claire knew, Eva was in Mia's arms, bouncing happily. "You look just like your cousin Valentina, yes you do," Mia cooed, wandering away.

Claire felt a little helpless, but she tried not to show it. It was Eva's family after all, and her daughter seemed pleased with the adoration. It was Claire who needed to adjust to her new reality. For the first time, it really hit her that she wasn't just bringing a father into Eva's life, she was bringing in his whole family. Eva would have an identity, a sense of belonging, other than Claire. The thought made her happy for her daughter and anxious for herself all at once. She always seemed to be the outsider, so this was no different.

"Would you like some wine, Claire?" Luca asked.

"Yes." Definitely. He poured her a glass and they all gathered on the couch. They chatted for a while, then Luca returned to the kitchen to finish off dinner, leaving the ladies alone for a few minutes.

"So, Luca didn't tell me much about you, just

the basics of how you two ended up having a child together. That's a pretty wild story."

"That's one way to put it."

"So if you don't mind me asking, what made you decide to go to a fertility clinic? My sister, Carla, was having some issues, too, but they were able to conceive with some medication. Now she's got three little hellions."

It seemed like a really personal question so early in the conversation, but she supposed that once everyone found out about Eva, it was a natural thing to ask. "My husband and I were having trouble and nothing was working, so we had to take the next step."

Mia's eyes widened, and she glanced at Claire's bare ring finger. "You're married?"

"Widowed."

Her hand clamped over her mouth. "I am so sorry." She turned to the kitchen. "Luca! Why didn't you tell me Claire was a widow and save me from asking a rude question?"

"I wouldn't have to if you weren't asking such nosy questions in the first place."

Mia muttered something in Italian under her breath. "I'm sorry. I was just curious about how all this came about. I know why Luca opted to go to the clinic, but not everyone has the same circumstances as he did, thankfully."

Claire perked up in her seat. She'd never directly asked Luca about his involvement with the clinic. Anytime the topic came up, he circumvented it somehow. She had no idea why a young, vibrant man would have stored his future chance at children at the clinic. Perhaps his sister could shed some light on the subject.

"I was so young at the time, but Mama told me how much he went through. She just hated to have him miss his chance at a family, too."

"Dinner!" Luca shouted with a large pasta platter in his hands.

Of course. Claire wasn't sure if Luca heard his sister talking or the timing was unfortunate, but the discussion came to a quick end with her once again not finding out the whole story about Luca. It was more than she knew before, though. He'd apparently had some kind of ordeal that might cost him a future with a family. Had he been ill? There wasn't anything lacking in the physical specimen she'd touched in the kitchen a few days ago. If he had been sick, it was a long time ago.

They gathered at the dining-room table with Eva in her high chair. She enjoyed a pouch of turkey and potato mush while the rest of them happily devoured the chicken tetrazzini. It was creamy and savory with the bite of parmesan and the fresh snap of the peas.

An hour passed as quickly as the first few minutes. Claire wasn't sure if it was the wine or Mia's easy nature, but before long they were chatting and laughing like old girlfriends. It was a relief for her, since she didn't have many friends and thought it might be a struggle. Mia was quite charming. They stayed mum on the topic of Luca, but since Mia had minored in art in college, she and Claire had a lot of other things they could discuss instead.

"He looks pouty," Mia said at last as she looked

at her brother. "We should probably talk about something he likes."

Claire turned to Luca, who was politely, yet blankly, sipping his wine and listening to them chat.

He shook his head in protest. "No, please. I'm fascinated by the female bonding ritual. As long as you stay off the subject of female biological processes and grooming, I'm fine."

"Now that you mention it, I am cramping pretty badly today," Mia said.

Luca immediately stood up and started clearing plates. "And I'm out," he said.

Mia laughed and picked up a few of her own. "I'm just messing with you, *fratello*. Carla and I used to do that to the boys when they were pestering us," she explained to Claire. "I once chased Marcello and Giovanni through the house with a box of tampons. You'd have thought it was a snake."

"They would've preferred a snake. See, Claire, what you avoided by being an only child? We tortured one another until we moved out of the house."

"That didn't stop us, really. Angelo texted me a picture of a giant spider the other day. I swear that thing was bigger than my hand. My skin was crawling for hours."

Claire followed them into the kitchen and couldn't help the amused smile on her face. She didn't know what Luca was talking about. She hadn't avoided this by being an only child, she'd missed out on it. It was different, for sure, but she enjoyed the camaraderie Luca and Mia had. She'd never had that with anyone.

As she handed off her plate and the salad bowl to Luca, she realized, sadly, that Eva would likely have the same fate. She would have the benefit of all of her cousins on Luca's side, but there would be no siblings to play with or talk to around the dinner table.

Eva had been a miracle, but in that moment, she felt greedy enough to hope that she would be granted one more.

Seven

"When you said you got a babysitter and were taking me out today, I kind of imagined things going differently."

Luca laughed at Claire and pulled the Land Rover into the dim parking lot of the marina. It was just before sunrise, and the sky was a dusky gray with a hint of pink on the horizon. "What were you expecting?"

"I don't know. A spa day? Maybe a nice dinner or walking around town shopping. At the very least, leaving the house after the sun had risen."

"We may still do all that. We've got all day."

Claire glanced at her watch and nodded. "We certainly do." She looked out at the boats in the marina with a curious expression. "Are we getting on a boat?"

"Maybe." Luca parked the car and got out. When he opened the door to let Claire out, her frown was pinching her brows together. "Okay, yes. We're going out on a boat. You really don't like surprises, do you?"

"It's not that I don't like them, per se, I'm just not used to them. At least not good ones."

"I'm going to change that." Luca took her hand and led her to the dock. There, waiting for them, was a small crew on a catamaran.

"Good morning, Mr. Moretti. Are you ready to go see some whales today?"

Claire's eyes were wide as she took the sailor's hand and climbed onto the deck of the ship. "We're going whale watching?"

"That's where I'm going," the captain said. "Since you're on my ship, that means you are, too. We're about to head out into some of the best and most diverse waters for marine life.

If all goes well, we should see humpbacks, fin whales, a couple species of dolphins and, maybe if we're lucky, a right whale. It feels like a lucky morning."

Luca watched as the captain joined his crew in readying the ship for departure. "Have you ever done something like this before?" he asked Claire.

"No," she said as she looked out at the gray waters. "I'm really excited, though. Are we waiting for some other passengers?"

Luca shook his head and turned back to watch the crew untie the mooring and start the engines. "No, it's only going to be us this morning. I reserved it just for you and me."

Her eyes widened with surprise. "Just for us?" She looked around the ship. "That's crazy."

"I told you," Luca explained, "that I wanted to take you out today so you could relax and enjoy yourself. Yes, I could take you to dinner or to a day spa, but I wanted to do something different."

As the boat started to pull out of the marina, one of the crew brought them a flannel blanket.

"Have a seat on the bench up front for the best views. Wrap up and I'll bring out some coffee and fresh baked cinnamon rolls."

They took their seats, and Luca wrapped the blanket around them. He put his arm around Claire's shoulders and pulled her to his side. She snuggled happily against him, resting her head on his shoulder. It was amazingly easy to be here with her like this. She seemed to fit perfectly in the crook beneath his arm, as if she was meant to be there.

Taking a deep breath, he drew in the salty scent of the air as it mingled with Claire's fragrance. Luca leaned in closer, pressing his lips into the crown of her head with a sigh. Combined with the gentle rocking of the ship, it was incredibly soothing.

After about ten minutes of quietly cutting through the calm seas, the crewman brought them coffee and warm, gooey cinnamon rolls. They ate quietly as they watched the sea around them. They were just finishing up when one of the crew shouted, "Two o'clock!"

Luca and Claire both stood and turned in the direction he was pointing. The sky was lighter now, burning away the early-morning fog. They could just make out the spray of a whale surfacing in the distance, followed by a dark hump rising out of the water. A few minutes later, they were rewarded with a stunning sight as the humpback whale leaped from the water and crashed back down in a spectacular splash.

Luca tried to focus on the amazing sight, but his gaze kept drifting back to Claire. She was totally immersed in the moment, her lips parted softly in unexpressed awe. This moment was memorable, but more so because she was here with him.

Lifting the blanket, he wrapped it around himself, then Claire, snuggling her back against his chest. She leaned into him, her eyes never leaving the water. They stood like that for nearly an hour, watching a pod of dolphins go by and one whale after the other surface. They didn't spot an elusive right whale, but they saw a pair of fin whales and a couple more humpbacks. The whales didn't breach again, but he and Claire were entertained with displays of tail lobbing and slapping of their pectoral fins on the water.

As the ship headed back to the marina, Claire turned in his arms to face him. "That was incredible," she said. "It's the most beautiful thing I've ever seen."

"They were amazing, but they weren't the most beautiful thing I've seen."

Claire snorted at him. "I'm sure being a billionaire has opened doors to plenty of things more beautiful than this, but this is probably as good as it gets for me. Second only to seeing Eva for the first time."

"My money has nothing to do with it," Luca argued. "In fact, most of the things I see in my day-to-day life are quite tedious. At least until I met you. You are by far the most beautiful thing I've ever seen."

Claire squirmed uncomfortably. "Luca…" she complained, but he wouldn't let her.

Luca pressed a finger to her lips and shook his head. "No. No arguing with me. I know better what I've seen and what I think than you do, thanks."

Her cheeks flushed pink and her eyes focused on his chest. "I'm sorry," she said. "I'm just not used to hearing things like that. It never feels sincere to me."

"I know, you've told me that before, but you need to get used to it because I'm not about to stop. I never say anything I don't mean, *tesorina*, so accept a compliment for what it is. If I say you're beautiful and I desire you above all else, I mean it."

Her mouth fell open again. Her gray eyes, so much like the water around them, met his. "You desire me?"

"I said it, didn't I?"

"I know." Claire bit at her lip, a line of concern forming between her brows. "I just can't help but wonder if a physical relationship between us is a bad idea."

"It probably is," Luca said with a laugh. "I told you I was honest, Claire, not smart."

* * *

"I don't know how I'm ever going to adjust to real life again."

Luca laughed at Claire as he unlocked the door of the house. "How's that?"

As though he didn't know what he'd done. "You've utterly spoiled me for reality. You take me to this beautiful island and let me spend my days listening to the waves and eating your amazing cooking. There's no alarm clocks, no bills to pay, no calls to take…"

They stepped into the house, shut the door behind them and slipped out of their coats. The cottage was dark and quiet, so Mia and Eva were already asleep. Luca wrapped an arm around her waist and pulled her close to whisper in her ear. "And what's wrong with that? You deserve to be spoiled."

Claire hesitated to respond as the heat of his touch burned through her dress. Her body was pressed provocatively against his. She wasn't sure if it was the physical contact or his seductive words, but suddenly the chill of the night was gone. A heat built deep inside her, spreading through her veins. She looked up at him, getting lost in his dark eyes.

"And then today…" she continued, pulling away and moving to the staircase.

"I thought you had a good time today," he said, following her upstairs.

"I had an excellent time today. The cruise and the whales were amazing. Walking around Edgartown and Oak Bluff was so relaxing. And then our meal at the Red Cat was some of the best food I've ever eaten."

Luca reached the top of the stairs and hesitated. An annoyed frown pulled down the corners of his mouth. "Better than my cooking?"

She wasn't getting caught in that trap. There was no right answer to that question. "They were completely different culinary styles. There's no comparison and I refuse to try."

Luca approached her again. This time, when he wrapped his arms around her waist, he held on tight enough for her to not escape so easily. Claire didn't shy away from his touch. Instead, she let herself melt into his body, each of her soft curves pressing into his hard muscles. She wouldn't lie to herself and say that it didn't feel good to be held.

She was beginning to wonder if Jeff had *ever* held her like this. The simple glide of Luca's hands over her back had more tenderness, yet more intensity, than any man who had touched her before. She felt sexy and alive with him, valued by him, and she hadn't felt that way in so long.

His dark eyes focused on her, making her wonder if he knew what she was thinking. His fingertips pressed into the flesh at her hips, leaving no doubt that he wanted her. They'd danced around this whole moment since they'd arrived at the island. Luca had gone out of his way to charm her, to reduce the stressors and barriers in her life that would keep her from enjoying herself. Claire had fought it the whole trip, but she was tired of fighting what she wanted. Now was her moment to indulge.

"Tell me, what is so bad about all of these

things I've done for you today? Am I not allowed to treat you to a nice time?"

"You can do whatever you like. It's just hard to have a day like that because I know this isn't what real life is like. Before too long, I'm going to go back to Brooklyn and cook my own dinner again. There won't be a beautiful beach out my window, and I won't wake up to the sound of waves crashing on the rocks."

"You can have anything you want. You just have to ask, *tesorina*."

She wondered what he meant by that. Her mind instantly leaped ahead to a life together, where he'd give her a beach house if that was what she wanted. That, of course, was a ridiculous fantasy brought on by their discussion on the boat and a little too much wine. He wasn't offering anything but an optimistic point of view. She decided to focus on something else instead, before she embarrassed herself. "Luca, what does *tesorina* mean?"

He smiled as he looked down at her. "It literally means *treasure* in Italian, but it's a term of endearment that is used like we would use sweetheart or honey in English."

Her breath caught in her throat when she heard the definition of the name he'd called her from their very first day together. "Why do you call me that?"

His brow furrowed. "Because that's what you are, Claire—both a treasure and the sweetest, most passionate creature I've ever met."

She couldn't hold back any longer. Those words were a stronger aphrodisiac than any food she could imagine. Lunging forward, she met his lips with her own. She wrapped her arms around his neck to tug him closer to her. Claire felt his hands glide over her rib cage and along her waist. She wanted more. She wanted him to touch her all over.

She pressed her body against his. She could feel the firm ridge of his desire pressing into her belly. Rubbing against it, she drew a low growl from Luca's throat. Feeling bold, she let her palm graze over his chest, dipping lower to stroke him through his pants.

Luca ripped his mouth from hers, reaching out quickly to grip her wrist and pull her away. "Claire," he nearly groaned. His whole body tensed as he struggled to keep control. "Don't. I can't take it. I want you too badly."

"Then take me. Please, Luca. I want you to make love to me. I want you to show me what it feels like to be with a man who truly desires me."

She watched him close his eyes for a moment and draw a deep breath in through his nose. When his eyelids rose, there was a heat in his gaze.

Her hand was trembling as she reached for his. Before she lost her nerve, she turned and walked toward her bedroom. Mia had moved Eva's playpen into her room tonight, so they had the space all to themselves.

Without turning back to face him, she reached for her dress and started fumbling with the buttons down the front. Claire could feel the heat of Luca's body at her back, but he didn't touch her. At least, not yet.

She let the top of the dress slip from her arms to pool at her waist. Luca's breath was hot on her nape as he moved in closer and pressed a searing kiss on her bare shoulder. The contrast sent a shiver down her spine that met with his fingertips as he gathered the fabric in his hands and pushed it over her hips.

The sundress pooled around her feet, leaving her in nothing but her underthings. Claire held her breath as Luca unlatched her bra and slipped the straps from her shoulders. He let it drop to the floor, immediately covering both breasts with his hands.

Claire gasped and arched her back to press her body closer to his touch. She could feel her nipples tighten and harden as his fingertips stroked over them. He continued to sprinkle kisses across her bare shoulders and neck, the combination of touches building a raging fire in her belly.

"Luca," she gasped as he rolled the peaks between his fingers. She wasn't entirely sure what she was begging him for, but she knew he could give it to her.

He responded by gliding his palm across her bare belly to the edge of her panties. She tensed as he moved over the skin that hadn't quite bounced back from having Eva, but he didn't seem to notice. Luca was focused on his destination. Without hesitating, his hand slipped beneath the satin and stroked across her sensitive center.

Claire gasped, but his firm grip on her body wouldn't allow her to squirm away from the intensity of his touch. *"Sì, bella,"* he cooed in her ear from behind as he moved relentlessly over her slick skin.

She felt her thighs start to tremble beneath her. Claire wasn't certain how much of this she could take. She might collapse into a puddle right there at his feet. "Not yet," she whispered between ever more urgent cries.

To her relief and disappointment, he pulled his hand away before it went too far. Instead, he hooked his thumbs around her panties and pulled them down her legs. Now she was completely naked. Thankfully, she wasn't alone in that. She heard the rustle of fabric behind her and turned in time to see Luca slip out of his shirt.

She reached for his belt and unfastened his pants. Luca stepped out of his remaining clothes and took a step toward Claire until their naked bodies were just barely brushing each other. He cupped her face in his hands and dipped his head to kiss her.

His desire for her was barely restrained as his mouth met hers. This was a kiss that had built up during their time together here. His tongue sought hers, tasting and teasing her with his lips. Claire met his intensity, nipping playfully at his bottom lip. The bite elicited a growl in the back of his throat. He moved his hands to her hips and slowly guided her backward through the room until she fell onto the bed.

Claire crawled across the mattress until she could lie comfortably. Luca followed her, kissing and touching every inch of her as he moved up the length of her body. He paused to hover

over her, his erection pressing insistently against her inner thigh. He lowered his head to kiss her again, then stopped.

Looking down at Claire, there was a flash of panic in his eyes. "Please tell me you have a condom with you."

A condom? Claire froze at the thought. She didn't have any. She hadn't used them since before she got married. "I don't. Don't you?"

"No, I didn't exactly plan for this to happen. Hold on," he said, climbing from the bed and dashing into her bathroom. "Bless you, Gavin," he shouted before returning to the bed with a foil packet in his hand.

Claire finally let out the breath she'd been holding. Thank goodness. She didn't want to stop now. Even the slightest hesitation might let reality rush in and ruin the moment. The odds of them conceiving were virtually nil, considering they'd met via a fertility clinic, but that wasn't the only worry. It had been a long time since she'd dated, but there had been plenty of things to catch then and now.

She dropped her head to the pillow as Luca sheathed himself and returned to his place between her thighs.

"Now, where were we?" he asked with a grin.

Claire reached between them and wrapped her fingers around his length. She pulled him just to the point of penetration and stopped. "Right about there, I think."

Luca nodded and pressed forward slowly. Claire closed her eyes, absorbing the feeling of having a man inside her after so long. Her muscles tightened around the invasion, making Luca hiss and clench his teeth as he buried himself fully inside her.

He continued moving at a slow and deliberate pace, drawing out the pleasure. Claire had been nervous about doing this after all this time, but that faded away once he touched her. She drew her legs up to cradle his hips between her thighs and let her body rock back and forth with his movements. The feelings he created radiated through her like shock waves of pleasure.

It wasn't until she opened her eyes again that

she realized Luca was watching her. Not just looking at her, but taking in everything. Seeing the pleasure dance across her face seemed to turn him on and make him bolder. He slipped a hand between their bodies and stroked between her thighs. Claire gasped, writhing beneath him as his fingers pushed her closer and closer to the edge. The more near her release came, the more forcefully Luca moved into her, making the climax build inside her even faster.

Luca had some kind of power over her. He seemed to know just how to touch her, just how to coax every sensation from her body in a way that should take a man time to master. All she could do was bite her lip and brace herself for it.

Then it hit her. The dam holding back the pleasurable rush inside her burst and she was swept up in it. "Luca!" she cried out, gripping at the sheets, but they failed to keep her from practically rising up off the bed.

Luca slowed down as Claire collapsed onto the pillows with heavy breaths. She felt as if all her energy had been zapped away, and she didn't care.

He lowered himself onto his elbows, burying his face in her neck. The stubble of his beard scratched against her skin as he rocked against her and whispered into her ear. "Watching you come undone like that... *Sei così bella*, Claire," he said. *"Ti voglio così male."*

She had no idea what he said, but the curly, seductive words sounded so wonderful. "Yes," she replied. "It's your turn, now."

Luca nipped gently at her shoulder, then dragged his lips across her throat before kissing her again. His gaze narrowed its focus on her again and one hand planted firmly on the curve of her hip. His fingertips dug into her flesh as he moved harder and faster than ever before. Claire felt every muscle in his body tense and at the last moment, his eyes finally squeezed shut. He roared as he poured into her with one final, powerful thrust.

And then he became unnaturally still in the thrill of the moment. She expected him to collapse or roll away, but he seemed to just freeze in place.

"What's the matter?"

He swallowed hard, his throat the only set of muscles he allowed to move. "I think the condom has broken." Luca reached over to the nightstand and picked up the wrapper. "You've got to be kidding me," he shouted, tossing it to the floor in anger. "This expired over a year ago."

In a rush, Luca pulled away and before she could stop him, he disappeared into the bathroom and shut the door. Claire sat awkwardly on the bed, not quite sure what to do. Her first foray into a renewed sex life had suddenly gone off track without warning. She clutched the sheets protectively to her chest, ignoring the pleasurable pangs that still echoed through her body.

Luca came out a few minutes later with a tortured expression pinching his face. "It did break. I'm sorry, Claire. I should've looked at the expiration date. I was just so desperate to have you that I didn't even think to look."

Claire was pretty sure there'd never been a

man so desperate for her that he would forget something like that. She wasn't about to beat him up over it. There wasn't much they could do now, anyway. "Don't worry about it. I mean, I doubt I'll end up pregnant, if that's what you're concerned about. It took me years and a medical intervention the last time. And I'm clean. They did all sorts of testing at the clinic and I haven't been with anyone since then."

"I'm not insinuating that you weren't clean or even worried you'd get pregnant. That would take a miracle." Luca slipped into the bed beside her and pulled her into his arms. "I've just never had one break before, so I'm a little rattled. It's always been a hard and fast rule of mine to wear one. I've never been with a woman without it. I'm sorry."

Claire nestled into his chest, feeling a little better now that he hadn't fled the room like the scene of a crime. "You didn't know it would break. Everything will be fine, I'm sure of it."

Luca brushed her damp hair from her face and held her close. "You're probably right. Let's just put it out of our minds and get some rest. Tomorrow, I'll go to the store."

"The store?" Claire questioned.

"To buy a box of new ones. I've only just begun to worship this body, *tesorina*."

Eight

This was nice.

With his nose buried in Claire's neck, the scent of cinnamon and vanilla filled Luca's lungs. His arm curled around her, holding her warm, soft body against his. He didn't want to move. He could just lie like this for hours.

It had been a long time since Luca had woken up with a beautiful woman in his arms. His plan to woo Claire had worked even better than he'd expected. If every time was as good as last night, he'd happily propose to her right now. Not even the condom debacle could ruin his good mood.

Then a sound stopped him cold. At first, he thought he was imagining things. The echo of his mother's voice was so completely out of context that it couldn't possibly be what he heard. Just when he'd convinced himself it was his imagination, Luca caught the unmistakable sound of his mother's laughter.

No. It *couldn't* be.

Luca heard Eva squeal with amusement and the chorus of cooing voices that could only be members of his family. He groaned and pulled away from Claire, sitting up in bed. She stirred beside him, looking over her shoulder with squinted eyes.

"What's the matter?" she asked in a low, sleepy voice.

Luca wasn't quite sure how to break the news, so he just spit it out. "I think…my family is here."

Claire rolled onto her back and sat up, clutching the sheets to her bare chest. She looked so messy and vulnerable, so unlike the put together woman who stomped into his lawyer's office.

He loved knowing both sides of this complex woman. Had he woken under any other circumstances, he would cover her body with his own and make love to her again. Instead he had to explain to her how his family had just crashed their beach vacation.

"You mean your sister?" she asked.

Luca swallowed hard and shook his head. "No, more than that."

The sound of his mother's laughter reached his ears again. When he turned to look at Claire, her sleepy expression was replaced with one of sheer panic. "Are you kidding me?"

"I wish I were. I think our secret is out. And that means Mia is in a lot of trouble."

Flinging back the blankets, Luca reached for his pants and tugged them on. He needed to go out there and figure out exactly what the hell was going on. He opened the door, completely dumbfounded by what he saw. In the center of the living room, his mother was holding up Eva as if she'd gotten her hands on the Holy Grail. His father was standing behind her, making faces at the baby until she squealed with delight. That was bad enough. Then, just beyond them, he saw Mia talking to his other sister, Carla. No fewer than five children were running around the living room, seeking excitement and hell-bent on destruction. He could already tell that he would have to write Gavin a fat check for everything they broke.

Luca turned just in time to see his youngest brothers, Giovanni and Angelo, come up the stairs with their wives. They were all carrying suitcases. That was a bad sign. This wasn't an afternoon visit. They were staying. What the hell was going on?

"Luca! You're awake!" his mother exclaimed.

"Do you really think I could sleep through all this?" He didn't even bother to mask his irritation. "What are you all doing here?" he asked with a pointed glance at Mia. His sister slunk behind Carla with a sheepish expression on her face. "And why, in God's name, do you have luggage?"

"You with all the questions," his mother

snapped. She curled Eva to her chest and narrowed her gaze at him. "I've got a question for you, young man! How long were you going to keep our new grandchild from us?"

"A little longer than this," his muttered under his breath. "How did you find out?"

"It's my fault," Mia admitted, as though there were another choice. "Well, actually, it was Eva's fault."

"You're blaming the baby?" Luca asked with incredulity in his voice.

"Yes and no. Carla called me last night while you and Claire were at dinner. I shouldn't have answered the phone, but I did. While we were on the phone, Eva started to cry. What was I supposed to tell her?" Mia asked. "I couldn't think of a good lie fast enough, so I told her the truth and then swore her to secrecy."

"So naturally, when I got off the phone I immediately called Mama," Carla said, confirming his logic on not telling her in the first place. "This wasn't the kind of secret you keep, sorry."

"She was right," his mother, Antonia, chimed

in. "How could you keep this beautiful little girl from us? Especially after everything you went through with Jessica."

"Because I've just found out about her myself," Luca said, scooping up the child from his mother and clutching Eva protectively to his chest. "And after what *did* happen with Jessica, I wanted to be sure before I told anyone. Once I got the test results, I selfishly chose to get to know Eva and her mother before all *this* happened."

His mother's hand came up to her mouth. "You don't even know the mother? At least with Jessica you two seemed to really be building toward a future together. I thought I taught you better than that, Luca. You're supposed to be a gentleman."

Luca sighed and rolled his eyes. "It wasn't like that. Mama, you know I can't…" He couldn't even say it aloud. He didn't need to. His whole family knew the truth, anyway.

"It was an accident at the fertility clinic," a woman's voice said from behind him.

Luca turned to see Claire standing in the doorway of the bedroom. In a matter of minutes, she'd dressed and transformed back into the prim and put together Claire he knew. Her dark blond hair was twisted into a bun, and her lips and cheeks were pink with a touch of makeup. She was wearing another sundress that looked amazing on her figure.

"Mama, Dad, everyone…this is Claire Douglas, Eva's mother."

"Oh, Luca." Antonia made a beeline for Claire, pulling her into a huge embrace. *"Lei è bella."*

Claire flinched slightly at the unexpected physical contact, but Luca could tell she was trying to play it off. She'd better get used to it. His whole family was very physically affectionate.

"Hello," she managed with a soft smile as his mother finally pulled away.

"It's so good to meet you, Claire. I'm sure we would've met sooner if I'd known you and Eva existed." There was a biting tone at the end of his mother's words directed at Luca. He didn't care.

"Claire, this is my family. That's my mother, Antonia. This is my father, Mario." He went around the room as fast as he could. She likely wouldn't remember all the names anyway. "You know Mia, then my sister Carla. My brother Giovanni and his wife, Nicole. My other brother Angelo and his wife, Tonia. My nephews Tony, Giovanni Jr., Matteo, Paolo and my niece Valentina."

Luca watched Claire's eyes get wider with every name he listed. "Is that everyone?" she asked.

"No," he had to admit. "My brother Marcello and his family apparently couldn't come, but they have a new baby. And it looks like Carla's husband stayed home with the kids." Luca turned his back to his family and silently mouthed the words to Claire, "I'm so sorry."

She just shook her head and pasted on a smile. "So glad all of you could come. Please, set down your things and relax. Can I get anyone something to drink? I was just about to make some breakfast. Have you eaten?"

The resounding roar of voices startled Claire for a moment, but Luca felt a touch of pride as she recovered. At the mention of food or drink, half the family headed toward the kitchen. No one bothered to tell her what they'd like; they simply took over like they would at home. She watched them for a moment in confusion.

Luca handed Eva to her and leaned over to whisper in her ear. "Just go with it. This is how they are." He leaned in to plant a kiss under her earlobe, but she shied away, heading toward the kitchen to help the others. He tried not to frown at her rejection.

Instead, he approached Giovanni as he sat in one of the overstuffed chairs. "Really?" he asked.

Giovanni just shrugged him off. "You know how they are. I got a phone call at ten last night telling me that you had a daughter and I was to be packed, ready and at the airport by six a.m. to go see her."

Luca slipped into the chair beside him. "You all took the corporate jet?"

His brother nodded. "Did you really think you could keep this a secret?"

"It worked for a few months."

"Months?" Giovanni looked stunned.

"Yes. I found out about this mistake at the clinic, and then I wanted to wait to get the results of the paternity test. You remember what happened with Jessica. I wanted to keep it under wraps until I knew for certain Eva was truly mine. After that were a few weeks of battling back and forth with her lawyer before I could see Eva. We came here to break the ice and figure out how to work together. It didn't seem like the right time to bring all of you into the picture."

"It seems understandable, but I doubt Mama will accept your excuse. Expect a tongue-lashing later."

Luca chuckled. "You mean that wasn't it just now?"

"Oh, no. You were saved by your pretty girlfriend and talk of cooking. That distracted her. You'll hear more about it when she's done pumping Claire for details and we've all been fed."

"She's not really my girlfriend," Luca argued. The way she pulled away from him a moment ago made that very clear. Last night was what it was, but she obviously didn't want his family to read into anything. "I mean, we're just…"

"You two came out of the same bedroom, Luca. And you're not wearing a shirt."

Luca looked down and realized he needed to fetch his shirt from the bedroom floor. "Yeah, but that was the first time. I'm not sure it will happen again, especially with you all showing up and breaking the romantic spell I'd so carefully crafted."

"Are you trying to woo her?" Giovanni asked.

"Not at first, but then I realized Claire and Eva might be my one shot at a real family. I'd be stupid to let this chance slip through my fingers."

"You don't know that for sure, Luca. Have the doctors—"

"No," Luca interrupted. "But *I* know. This is my chance. It could be worse. Claire is…" He found it hard to find the words in the moment. "A very special woman. And a great mother."

The two brothers turned to look into the kitchen. Their parents, Mia, Carla, Nicole and

Angelo were talking all at once, bumping elbows and carrying around ingredients for the breakfast of champions. Tonia was unsuccessfully trying to corral a toddler. Claire stood on the fringe with Eva, not quite brave enough to jump in. She watched the group with fascination, like a circus performance.

Periodically, their mother would stop what she was doing to pat Claire's arm and pinch at Eva's cheeks. She'd mutter something in Italian that they couldn't make out, then she'd return to what she was doing.

"Well, dating or not, Mama seems to like Claire," Giovanni noted. "That's a huge hurdle to get over."

Their mother was notoriously picky about the women her sons dated. It was a pretty big deal to get the Antonia Stamp of Approval. Luca had never brought a woman home before Jessica, and that was only because of the baby. Even without Eva, Luca got the feeling that his mama would take to Claire. It was hard not to like her, even as different as she was.

"Does she know about your illness?" Giovanni asked.

Luca stiffened in his seat and shook his head. "No. And I don't want anyone telling her, either."

"It's not a big deal, Luca. You had cancer. That's nothing to be ashamed of. You survived. You should be shouting it from the rooftops."

Luca knew his brother was right, but he'd never felt like shouting. He only ever felt as if he'd lost something. A woman like Claire deserved a whole man who could give her everything she wanted.

Maybe, just maybe, he could fake it and be enough for her.

Overwhelmed wasn't quite the word Claire would use to describe the past three days, but it was close. She knew now what Luca was talking about when he said his family was loud, boisterous and fun-loving. They were all of those things and more. The sisters and sisters-in-law had taken Claire into their fold. She was worried they would be cold to her when they found out about the custody battle she and Luca had been fighting, but that wasn't the case. They'd taken the children to the beach and the ice-cream stand. They'd sat out on the deck together drinking wine and talking about children and men. It was surprising how quickly the sense of camaraderie had set in with these women who were virtual strangers.

Claire had barely even seen Eva since they arrived. Someone was always holding her. The only time they'd had together was when she would insist on giving Eva a bath and putting her to bed. Her room was her only sanctuary. There were Morettis everywhere else. The three couples took over the downstairs bedrooms with the kids sleeping on the floor in blanket forts. Mia and Carla shared the sofa bed.

Truthfully, there was a Moretti in her room, too, but it wasn't quite the same. She had let Luca return to her room while they were there, but only because there wasn't anywhere else to sleep. She felt guilty taking up a king-size bed while he tried to get rest on the recliner. She'd set a few rules, however. No hanky-panky. There were too many people around to hear every creak in the wood floors.

Besides that, she wasn't sure it was something that should be repeated, as much as she might like to. Luca was a complex man, and she got the feeling it would take a long time to peel back all his layers. Sex was just a distraction. If she was going to fully give herself to anyone, there had to be a level of trust and honesty between them. She didn't feel as if she and Luca had that yet. And maybe they never would. This trip wasn't supposed to be about romance anyway. It was supposed to be about family, and now, it certainly was.

On the third afternoon of his family's visit, the men had all gone out in search of fresh lobster to bring home for dinner. Mia and Carla had gone to the grocery store to replenish the pantry they'd depleted. Nicole and Tonia went to the beach with the kids, but Claire passed. She was exhausted from all the activity.

Suddenly, the house felt very quiet. Too quiet.

After a while, she started to wonder where Eva was. Although she rarely had her, she did like to keep tabs on where she was. Claire meandered through the house, finally spying her out on the deck with Antonia. She slipped through the French doors and approached the deck chairs.

"May I join you?" she asked.

"Of course. My new grandbaby and I were just enjoying this beautiful day. I'm going to hate to leave tomorrow. I have so much more sugar to give these little cheeks."

Claire sat down and watched as Eva's face lit up at her grandmother's sweet baby voice and kisses. She was really blossoming with all this attention. Perhaps not putting her in day care where she could be around a lot of different people was a bad idea. She was alone with Daisy all day, but Eva really seemed to like people. Perhaps she was more Moretti than Douglas.

"Claire, since everyone is gone at the moment, I wanted to talk to you about something. Being alone is a luxury in my family, so I've learned to take full advantage of it when it comes."

Claire bit her bottom lip to hide her frown. That sounded ominous. Was this the part where she threatened Claire not to hurt her son or keep his daughter from him? Told her to call off her lawyer? "Sure."

"I'm not sure what it is you and Luca have going. I know that whatever it is, it's early, so it's hard to say whether or not what you two have will turn into something serious, but I hope it does. I have never seen Luca as happy as he is here with you and Eva. Not even with Jessica was he like this. With her, he always seemed to be waiting for the other shoe to fall, and of course in the end he was right."

Claire wanted to push Antonia for more information, but she held her tongue, deciding not to interrupt.

"It broke my heart to see him like that. Finding out he had a child was such a startling revelation, but then he really warmed up to the idea. He was excited and nervous, but as he always does, Luca held back. We never expected to find out that the baby wasn't his."

Claire tried to hide her surprise at this revelation about Luca. He'd never once mentioned this other child or its mother. Even if it wasn't his in the end, that was an important event in his life he'd kept from her. She closed her eyes as all the pieces started to fall into place. That explained why he was so adamant about claiming Eva as his own. This time, he was certain the baby was his and he wasn't going to miss his chance to be a father, no matter what the circumstances.

"But this child," Antonia continued with a smile, "is the miracle that will bring him back to life. Whether or not he thought it would happen, he finally has a family."

"He has a daughter, yes," Claire clarified. She wasn't quite ready to commit to more than that. "And I'm going to make sure he has Eva in his life as much as he wants her to be."

Antonia's golden hazel eyes, so much like Luca's that it made her a little uneasy, fixed on Claire. "Dear, you and I both know that he's got a little more than just a daughter out of this situation."

Claire bit at her bottom lip as she considered her answer. "I don't really know. Sometimes things are going well, and I think maybe something is happening between us. Then he pulls away. Knowing about the other child explains a lot, but not everything. I still feel like he's keeping things from me, and that's a deal breaker for me. I'm not going to let myself get invested in a man I can't trust."

"Luca is as good a man as they come. He's just afraid to let himself fall for a good woman. Personally, I think you two are meant to be together. I don't believe in accidents or coincidences. Fate stepped in and scrambled those numbers on the labels so two strangers could share a child, and eventually, a life together."

That was a nice thought, but Claire wasn't quite so superstitious. Accidents happened. That didn't mean it was fate. It was just rotten luck. Or even good luck. It might not be what she planned, but at least Eva had a father and a family now. But as for him and her? She doubted this little vacation romance would last all the way back to Manhattan if he continued keeping secrets.

Luca's mother thought he was a peach, of course, but mothers loved their children blindly. He had given Claire his body, but he was holding back everything else. Unless that changed, she couldn't trust him with her heart. She'd already made the mistake of giving that away too freely in the past.

Something would go wrong. The dull ache in her gut was evidence of that. The only question was how badly it would hurt her when it happened.

Nine

"It's too quiet around here," Claire said as she washed up the last of the dinner dishes.

Luca looked up from his spot on the living-room floor. He and Eva were having fun with some fabric blocks with little tags on the edges. Frankly, he couldn't understand the appeal. He cut the tags off every piece of clothing he owned, but babies seemed completely enamored with them.

"I know what you mean," he said. His family had left a few days earlier. After three solid days of big Italian family chaos, the house almost seemed to echo with emptiness. "It always takes me a while to adjust to being alone again after we have get-togethers. Does that mean you like my family?"

Luca wasn't quite sure how his quiet, reserved Claire would handle Mia, much less the whole crew at once, but she'd done amazingly well. She fit in better than he'd ever expected. Whether or not she enjoyed her time with them was still a mystery to him, however.

Claire pulled the drain plug in the sink and strolled back into the living room while she dried her hands with a dish towel. "I love your family, Luca. They're amazing. I didn't even know a family could be like that. It's mind-boggling, really. I mean, they'd just met me and they treated me like family. Jeff's family was always kind to me, but I never felt like I was one of their daughters, even when legally I was."

Luca smiled at her. "They really liked you. I'm pretty certain they aren't like that with everyone. Even Carla liked you, and she's pretty hard to win over. And Mama. Well, you could do no wrong in her eyes. If you spoke Italian, you'd be perfect. Maybe we can work on that," he added with a grin.

"Very funny," Claire said as she sat down on the couch.

He turned back to Eva in time to see her let out a big yawn. "Uh-oh. I think she is ready for bed."

"Like me, I think she's still recovering from all the overstimulation."

Claire moved to get up, but Luca raised his hand. "You relax. I'll put her to bed. Why don't you pour us some wine, if my sisters didn't drink it all."

Luca stood and lifted Eva into his arms. Her little eyes kept slowly closing, then startling open as she tried to keep herself awake. "Don't fight it, *bella.*"

It only took a few minutes to change the baby, put her into her pajamas and settle her into her crib. He turned on the mobile overhead and ran his hand over her soft baby curls. *"Buona notte, cara mia."*

Eva cooed at him for a moment, then her eyes fluttered closed. That was quick. Slipping out quietly, he closed the bedroom door behind him. "You know," he said, "it's almost time to go back to New York and we haven't done the one thing we said we came here to do."

Claire glanced up at him from her spot on the sofa with a curious look. "What's that?"

"Discuss the custody arrangement we want to submit to the judge."

An odd expression flickered in her eyes. Luca couldn't tell if it was disappointment, fear, anxiety or a combination of all three. "Okay. Let's discuss it, then."

Luca crossed the living-room floor and settled on the couch beside her. "Have you had a chance to review the proposal that Edmund sent up here with me?"

"Yes, I looked it over. There wasn't a lot that concerned me. I was surprised, honestly. It seemed pretty standard to me, and after the time we've spent here, I think most of my worries about your abilities as a father have been addressed. I only had one question. The child support seemed a little high to me."

Luca's brow went up. "High? I'm sure that's the first time anyone's ever heard that." He wondered, sometimes, if Claire underestimated just how much he was worth. Any other woman would've done her research and milked him for every penny.

Claire shrugged off his comment. "Even if I put her in one of the best schools in Manhattan and dressed her in designer clothes, I wouldn't need that much each month. We have a nice home, a caregiver. It makes me worry a little."

"About what?"

"That you're wanting more from me than the plan outlines. Is there an expectation that I should sell my brownstone and move to Manhattan? The expense of an Upper East Side apartment near you is the only thing I could imagine would justify the money."

The thought had crossed his mind a time or two, but he had learned early on that trying to push Claire would get him nowhere. He had to use his best negotiating skills to get what he wanted. "That wasn't my intention, no. But would it be so bad if I wanted that? You'd be closer to the museum. Closer to the schools we discussed. It would be easier on Eva to move back and forth between us, or for one of us to step in if the other needed them."

Luca watched the wheels silently turn in her head as he spoke. He knew it made sense, but he knew she also loved her place. "It's up to you, but as you said, that amount of money I'm offering you could easily make that a possibility."

She brushed a stray strand of honey blond hair from her face and nodded. "I'll have to think on that. I like being able to get away from the chaos of the city sometimes."

He laughed. "You act as though Brooklyn is in the middle of a hayfield. If you want, I'll buy a country house in Connecticut you can visit whenever you need to get away."

Claire's eyes widened. "Don't be silly."

Luca didn't think it was silly. It seemed completely practical to him. Despite all his planning to seduce Claire and lure her into a relationship while keeping himself emotionally removed, he'd failed miserably. He wasn't sure he'd call what he felt for her love, but he certainly felt more than he'd ever intended to.

At this point, he was willing to do almost anything it took to get Claire to play a bigger role in his life. Having her live nearby was just one part of that. If buying a country house helped his cause, so be it. He was dreading the end of this trip. He knew that returning home would mean long hours in the office, and, if he was lucky, seeing Eva every other weekend. That wasn't good enough for him, especially when nothing in the paperwork dictated how often he'd get to see Claire.

"Well, how about this? I've been thinking a lot about all of this the past few days since my family left. If I'm being honest, I don't want to let what you and I have started slip away. I want us to build on it. It's all new to me, this relationship stuff, but I want to know how much more we can have together. And maybe if that happens and goes well, all that paperwork and custody agreements won't matter anymore. I don't just want Eva in my life, Claire. I want you in my life, too."

Claire's mouth dropped open the way it always did when he stole her prepared words from her lips. After a moment, her jaw closed and she smiled. "I want you in my life, too, Luca."

Luca leaned into her, wiping away the smile with his kiss. The minute his lips met hers, he felt that familiar surge of need run though his body and urge him on. That touch, combined with being alone again in the house, reminded him just how long he'd gone without touching Claire the way he'd wanted to. While his family was there, she had kept her distance. Now that she'd agreed to be in his life for a while longer, he wanted her back in his bed, as well.

"Luca," Claire said as she pressed against his chest with the palms of her hands. "Wait. I'm glad you're happy, but I wasn't finished. There was a 'but' coming."

But? Luca sat back against the arm of the couch with a frown. "What's wrong?"

Claire sighed. "There's nothing wrong, per se, but I wanted you to know that your mother told me something while she was here."

Luca felt the dull ache of dread in his stomach. She hadn't… Who was he kidding? Of course she had. His mother never respected his desire to keep his private past private. "What did she happen to share?" he asked, knowing full well what the answer was—she knew he was a one-balled wonder and had reservations about the two of them together.

Claire's eyebrows drew together in concern. "She told me about Jessica and the baby. Primarily, the point was how happy you seemed and how she'd wanted it so badly after everything you went through with Jessica. It worries me, Luca."

Luca was surprised. He thought for sure his mother would've spilled the cancer story. Perhaps she'd finally agreed to let him put that behind him. He breathed a sigh of relief. "What worries you, exactly?"

"That you didn't tell me about it yourself," she said, surprising him. "Since we've been here, I've told you every secret I have. I told you about Jeff, about my feelings of inadequacy and my failing marriage. You had a million opportunities to open up to me about this, but you didn't."

"It didn't seem relevant," Luca said. "It turned out to be nothing. I don't have another child you don't know about, so I didn't think it would matter to you."

"It's not about the child, but that you kept it to yourself. Secrets worry me, Luca. Jeff kept secrets. And as much as I want you in my life and I want to see how far this can go, I need to know you're going to be honest with me, even when it's uncomfortable. Even when it might expose the ugly parts of ourselves that we don't want anyone to see. It concerns me that you don't trust what we have enough to share that with me. It makes me wonder what else you're keeping from me."

Luca started to open his mouth to insist he wasn't keeping things from her, but she held her finger to his lips. "Don't. Don't tell me you're not, because I know that you are. Tell me, Luca. Tell me why you were at the fertility clinic. What happened to you? Tell me right now or I can't move forward with this."

Luca sighed. He'd been dreading this moment since he'd decided to make a future with Claire. Things could go horribly wrong from here, but he got the feeling it would be worse to avoid her questions. As much as he didn't want to, he needed to tell this story at least one more time.

"When I was in high school, I was diagnosed with testicular cancer. I missed most of my junior and senior years going through treatment. I had to have surgery to remove the tumor along with one of my testicles, then I went through extensive radiation and chemotherapy. I donated at the fertility clinic before the radiation because I would likely be sterile afterward. That's why Jessica having my baby was such a huge deal to my family. I wasn't supposed to be able to have children. I don't like talking about it, so I avoided your questions about school earlier because it would lead into that topic. I didn't get to go to prom. I got my diploma in a wheelchair. That whole period of my life was defined by my illness."

Claire's expression crumbled into near tears as he told her the truth. He reached his arm out for her. "Come here," he said. Claire snuggled against him, and he wrapped his arm around her shoulders. With her beside him and her curious eyes turned away, it was easier for him to talk.

"Don't cry. I'm sorry. I should've told you about that, but it was so hard on me and I don't like reliving it. I was just a kid. Someone that age shouldn't have to worry about whether or not they can have children someday when they'd never even kissed a girl, much less face their own mortality. I wasn't sure if I was going to make it to my next birthday. The price of beating the cancer was high. It took more from me than a teenager my age could understand at the time. Even now, knowing what I do, I would pay it gladly, but it's not something that ever goes away. I've continued to pay to this day."

Claire could hear the pain in Luca's words and it made her heart break a little more the longer he spoke. He was right; that wasn't something a child should have to deal with.

"The physical toll was a lot to get over. I recovered from the surgery, my hair grew back after the chemo, but that really isn't the worst part of it all. The worst part is the waiting."

"Waiting for what?"

"Waiting for it to show up again."

She placed a reassuring hand on his knee. "You don't know that it will. It has been over ten years since you were sick. That's a long time to go. Don't you think if the cancer was going to come back it would have already?"

"Don't use logic in the same context as cancer. It doesn't work. Besides, I know that's not true. The treatment I received to destroy the cancer alone puts me at risk of developing a secondary cancer at some point. It also can cause a slew of other health issues later in life. I suppose I should be happy to have a 'later in life' to get sick from the long-term effects of the chemo and radiation."

"So is that why you've focused so much on work at the expense of your relationships? In case you got sick again?"

"In part," he admitted. "The children part doesn't help, either. I don't ever want a woman to give up her dream of a family because she had the misfortune of falling in love with me."

"Luca!" Claire said, sitting up to look him in the eye. "The woman who falls in love with you is anything but unfortunate. You have so much to offer. You're doing yourself a disservice by only focusing on what you can't do. Besides, there are plenty of women out there who already have children or don't want any. Or can't have any," she said with a pointed tone. "Like me."

Luca looked at her with dark eyes that reflected a pain he'd always hidden from her before. There was a vulnerability there that she never expected to see in the eyes of her confident CEO. She hated that he had been through such horrible things, but she was happy to finally feel the last walls coming down between them. He deserved to be happy.

And more than anything, she wanted him to be happy with her. Her defenses were coming down as quickly as his own. Before she could stop herself, she leaned into him, capturing his face in her hands before she pressed her lips to his.

The emotional current running through each of them connected with a spark of a desire. Luca's hands pulled her closer, his hungry mouth eager to pick up where they'd left off a few minutes ago. This time, Claire wasn't about to stop him. She eased into his touch, craving the feel of him against her.

It didn't take long for the throbbing ache of need to build inside her. Claire had been content enough to go without a man for months and months, but Luca had opened Pandora's box. She wanted him. Now.

Pulling on his shirt, Claire slipped down to the

rug and brought Luca with her. Their lips never parted as they slid to the floor. Luca's heavy body covered hers, the weight of it making her feel secure, somehow. She had been drifting through life since Jeff died, but here and now, she finally had an anchor to keep her steady.

"Make love to me, Luca," she whispered against his lips. "Let me show you that you're everything a woman needs."

Her words lit a fire in him, and she was happy to receive the results of it. His hands slid over her body, pulling at her cotton dress and exposing the length of her leg beneath it. He continued pushing the fabric up until it bunched around her waist.

He sat up then, abandoning her lips at last so she could pull his shirt over his head and toss it away. Her hands immediately moved to his chest, rubbing over the hard muscles. She let the smooth crescents of her fingernails drag over the ridges of his six-pack, leaving tiny half moon imprints just above the waistline of his jeans.

Before she could unbutton his fly, Luca moved out of her reach.

He traveled slowly down her body, leaving a trail of kisses across her bare skin. He pushed the straps of her dress off her shoulders and tugged at the neckline until her breasts spilled over the top. His mouth teased and tasted her, sucking hard at her puckered nipples until Claire cried out and buried her fingers in the thick waves of his hair.

The tiny fire he'd ignited in her had grown to a steady burn. She ached for him, tugging him close even as his touch was so intense that she was tempted to pull away. As the kisses moved across her stomach and he nipped at the quivering muscles of her inner thigh, she felt the need gnawing inside her with no release in sight.

With nimble fingers, Luca removed her panties. Claire sighed in relief, thinking she would finally have him, but she was wrong. His jeans were still firmly in place as he pressed her thighs apart. Her breath caught in her throat as she realized what he was doing.

"Luca?" she gasped.

He paused, looking up at her from between her thighs. "Yes, *tesorina*?"

"What are you…you're not…?" She couldn't even ask the question. Claire was embarrassed to admit that this was something she'd never experienced before. Jeff had felt it was unhygienic, although he never seemed concerned when he wanted *her* to satisfy *him*.

Luca narrowed his gaze at her just as her cheeks starting flaming with embarrassment. "What's the matter? Haven't you been pleasured like this before?"

She squeezed her eyes shut and shook her head. Claire heard only a low rumble of anger in Luca's throat.

"I see your bastard of a husband failed in yet another aspect of your marriage. I intend to rectify that right now."

Claire was torn. It seemed like an incredibly intimate thing. She wasn't certain if she was ready for something like that. "I don't know, Luca. I'm not sure I—"

Without warning, Luca's tongue flicked across her aching flesh and stole her protest. A bolt of pleasure like she'd never experienced before shot through her body. "Luca!" She gasped and arched her back off the plush living-room rug.

He waited until the muscles in her body relaxed again, then he stroked ever so slowly across her with his tongue. Claire bit at her lip to keep from shouting too loudly and waking up Eva. It was difficult, especially when Luca encircled the outside of her thighs with his arms, pressed his palms against her inner thighs and opened her even wider to him.

The sensations of the intimate caress made it easier to forget how awkward all this seemed. The touch of his silky tongue on her most sensitive parts brought her close to an intense climax far faster than she ever anticipated. She wiggled and writhed beneath him, feeling it building inside of her, yet being virtually helpless to do anything about it.

Luca eased up on her for a moment, then he pressed her knees back until they were pushed against her chest. She caught her legs behind each knee to hold them there. At least that gave her something to grasp at when he returned to her, this time with his hands free.

With renewed fervor, he devoured her. Claire could only chant "yes, yes" as he drove her closer and closer to the edge. At the perfect moment, he slipped a finger inside her and she was done. The most intense orgasm she'd ever experienced exploded. Tiny sparks of pleasure danced through her whole body as her muscles quivered and tightened.

Luca retreated, but Claire barely had the energy to open her eyes. She managed to do it just in time to see his jeans pile onto the floor and an empty condom wrapper follow it. He'd kept his promise and went to the store, even with his family's unexpected arrival.

"Keep your legs right there," he whispered as he returned to her.

Her overstimulated nerves lit up as he slowly pressed his length into her. With her legs back, he reached farther, deeper than she ever could've imagined possible. When he was finished, her knees were resting on his shoulders. She could barely catch her breath, but she didn't care. This is what she'd wanted, more than anything. She wanted to be one with him in a way she'd never been with anyone else.

Luca murmured soft words in Italian against the sensitive skin of her inner knee as he thrust into her again. Each movement was so slow, so deliberate, so tortuous, as though he didn't want it to end. She didn't want it to end, either.

Claire opened her eyes and watched his face as he moved so she would always remember this moment. His brows were drawn together in concentration, as though he were preparing an amazing dish in the kitchen, as if this were the most important task he'd ever completed. He made her feel that way, too—as though she was a priority in his life. She'd never had that before. She didn't want to let that go. Not at the end of this trip. Not after the judge's ruling. Not ever.

Because she was in love with him.

After what happened with Jeff, she told herself

she wouldn't make the mistake of falling in love again. You couldn't trust someone enough not to take your heart and soul and crush it. Claire refused to give someone that much power over her again, and yet here she was. It might not be the smart thing to do, and it might bring her nothing but heartache before it was through, but there was no fighting it any longer.

Claire could feel it down in her bones, down in her core. Even as another release built up inside of her, she knew the sensation couldn't begin to touch the feeling of love that was warming her heart.

"Yes!" she gasped over and over as she felt both of them tense with anticipation.

Yes, she was close to oblivion. *Yes*, he was doing everything right. *Yes*, she wanted him to lose himself in her. *Yes*, this was better than she could've ever dreamed. *Yes*, she wanted to be with him back in New York. *Yes*, she loved Luca with everything she was and everything she had.

Yes to it all. He needed only ask the question and she was his forever.

Ten

It felt strange to be back in New York. Despite Luca's assurances that he wanted their relationship to continue beyond their time at the beach, Claire was anxious stepping back onto the concrete of her home turf. Her stomach was constantly fluttering like butterflies had invaded. If she thought about it too long, she hovered on the verge of nausea. She wasn't quite sure what she was afraid of.

That was a lie. She knew exactly what she was afraid of—losing Luca. It was the risk she'd taken when she gave in to her feelings for him.

Manhattan didn't have the cozy charm of the island. Would they really be able to hold this relationship together among the honking cabs, demanding jobs and hectic schedules of real life?

Tonight, she would find out. They'd been home a few days. Today had been her first day back at the museum. Luca had asked her to dinner tonight so they could put together their final custody agreement for Edmund and Stuart to submit to the judge. She was supposed to meet him at his apartment, then they'd go somewhere for dinner when they were through. Daisy was staying late to watch Eva.

Luca's apartment was just a few blocks from the museum. She walked down the massive steps to head in that direction. It was a nice evening and she wanted to make the most of the pleasant weather. She was actually feeling pretty good tonight.

At least until she caught a whiff of the nearby hot-dog cart. Normally the smell didn't bother her—sometimes it was even enticing—but tonight it was anything but. She frantically sought out a nearby trash can and emptied the contents of her stomach into it.

When she was through, she straightened and clamped her hand over her nose and mouth. Had she really just done that? She looked around to see if anyone noticed. They had. She was getting more than a few disgusted looks from tourists and locals alike.

A nearby woman reached into her purse and handed Claire a tissue. "I don't know why they call it morning sickness," she said. "More like all the damn time sickness. Those hot-dog carts always got me, too. Don't let those people bother you. When you're bringing a child into the world, you have the right to puke wherever you need to."

Claire tried not to frown at the well-meaning woman. There was no sense in dumping her life story on her by arguing that she couldn't get pregnant. She just accepted the tissue and was thankful that at least one person wasn't judging her. "Thank you."

She dashed across the street when the light

changed and tried to put as much distance between her and the mess as she could. It wasn't until she reached the light at the next block that she hesitated and let the woman's words sink into her head.

Pregnant? She couldn't possibly be pregnant.

Admittedly, this did feel like morning sickness. When she was pregnant the first time, there had been days when she couldn't even get out of bed. She lost weight instead of gaining it. She went through a sleeve of saltine crackers a day. The misery of her first trimester was something she'd quickly put out of her mind as the price she paid for Eva, but in the moment it came rushing back with crystal clarity.

She pulled out her phone and looked at her calendar. Doing a little math, she realized that she'd been at the beach over a month and her period was well overdue. But that just had to be a fluke. Yes, as if her public vomiting was a fluke.

Claire crossed the street with the crowd again, feeling more and more anxious with every step. She didn't know why. It was likely the questionable chicken-salad sandwich she'd had at the museum cafeteria today. There was no way she was pregnant. Even if she *could* conceive normally and Luca *hadn't* had cancer, the condom had only broken once.

Once was all it took. The ominous words of her high-school sex-ed teacher haunted her.

There was no way she could march into Luca's apartment and act like nothing was wrong while this weighed on her mind. She also didn't want to bring up the possibility and raise both their hopes only to find out she was just perimenopausal with food poisoning. This was easily dealt with. She needed to buy a pregnancy test, take it and move on with her day without this uncertainty. It was a waste of ten dollars, but it was a small price to pay for peace of mind.

In the drugstore, she sought out the aisle she'd haunted while undergoing all those fertility treatments. She picked up her favorite brand and carried it to the counter. How many of these had she taken over the years? Dozens. Only one had ever come back positive. Tonight was probably not the night for a repeat.

After paying for it, she continued down the block to a Starbucks. It may not be her first choice for where to take a pregnancy test, but she had to know now, before she got to Luca's. She took it into the women's restroom, then nervously awaited the results. When the alarm on her phone went off, she finally let herself check the tiny window.

Pregnant.

Claire's jaw dropped open in surprise and shock. That was impossible. How could she...? It had only... She could barely complete a thought, much less a sentence. Putting the cap on, she slipped the test back into her purse and headed back to the drugstore to buy another one from a different brand, then repeated the test. The screen varied, but the results were the same— two lines instead of one.

Confused, she packed up her things and left. It took another block before the news really started to sink in. She was pregnant. After the years of

trying, the tests, the shots, the invasive procedures to conceive Eva…she'd managed to get
pregnant *accidentally*. She had prayed for another baby. Dreamed of it, knowing that the odds
of it happening were almost astronomical. And
now, if all went well, she was going to have one.
Eva would have a brother or sister, and she and
Luca would have a second child together. It was
a miracle.

The excitement was nearly bubbling out of her
as she entered his building and signed in at the
desk. When she got off the elevator, she had a
huge grin on her face. She couldn't suppress it
as much as she wanted to surprise him with the
news.

Luca opened the door. A curious expression
came across his face as he looked at her. "Hi.
What are you so happy about?" He stepped back
to let Claire inside and took her jacket.

"I have some news," she said. "Let's sit down
first."

Luca followed her over to the couch where they
sat together. She scooped up his hands in hers.

"I know that you and I have only been together a short while, and for anyone else, this might be an unwelcome development, but I haven't been feeling well since we got back. I hadn't thought much about it, but a lady outside the museum said something today that got me to thinking. On the way over here, I took a pregnancy test…"

Luca stiffened. Those were the last words he expected to come out of her mouth. Sitting up straight, he pulled his hands away from hers. "And?" he forced himself to ask, already knowing the answer. If it was negative she wouldn't have bothered mentioning it.

She reached into her purse and pulled out two pregnancy tests. "And it came out positive. Both of them. I'm pregnant. I could hardly believe it myself. It must've happened when the condom broke that first time."

Luca took one of the tests from her hand, studying the tiny screen and hoping for the information to change. It was happening again. The dull ache in his gut told him that much. What he didn't understand was why she would try this. She knew he couldn't have children. He'd told her that only a few short days ago. "It's not possible," he said.

"I know. That's what I thought. I mean, I would have thought it was impossible, which is why I ignored all the signs. I need to go to the doctor to confirm the results and check on everything, but—"

"No," he said, interrupting her stream of words. He couldn't stand to just sit there and listen to her prattle on when he knew in his heart it was all lies. The surprise, the excitement…it all had to be carefully crafted so he'd believe the child was his and not question it.

"What do you mean, no? You told me you wanted a family. Why are you so upset? I'm pregnant, Luca."

"I'm sure you are." He got up from his seat and walked out of the living room and into the kitchen. He needed a little space. He could feel the muscles in his neck and jaw tightening. Before too long, he'd have a raging headache.

Claire didn't take the hint. She followed him

through his apartment, a confused frown wrinkling her forehead. "I thought you'd be happy."

Luca chuckled bitterly and looked down at the pregnancy test in his hand. He'd made that mistake once; he wouldn't fall for it again. It was a false hope. Instead, he tossed the test into the trash can. "If I was the father, I would be happy. But like I said, that's impossible."

Claire froze in place, not quite sure she could believe the words he'd just said. "Luca, you are the father. Who else would it be?"

To be honest, he didn't really want to consider the possibilities. He was already fighting through this storm of emotions swirling inside him. He didn't need to add furious jealousy to the list. Luca narrowed his gaze at her. "I have no idea, but I'm pretty sure it's not the sterile guy in the room."

"Look, I'm as surprised as you are. Between the two of us and our issues, it never crossed my mind that it could happen, but it did. You are the baby's father. I've spent every day and night of the last month with you. The last man I was with before you died a year ago."

Luca wanted to believe her. God, he wanted to. Claire had never given him any reason not to believe what she said before. But this story was just too far-fetched. She did a good job seeming sincere, though. "That all sounds good, Claire. You must've practiced before you came over."

She flinched as though his sharp words were a slap across the face. "Practiced? Do you really think I'm making all this up?"

He wanted to say no, that he believed her and was happy, but he couldn't let himself do it. The anger he'd suppressed over the past decade bubbled inside him. There was no one he could blame for the cancer or the treatments. He couldn't direct that emotion at anyone. Jessica disappeared when the paternity results came back negative, so he never got to say what he wanted to say to her, either. But in that moment, Claire was a convenient target for the disappointments of his life.

"No," he replied coolly. "Just the part where

I'm the father. What I can't seem to figure out was where you got the time to sleep with someone else."

Luca watched Claire's face turn red and the vein in her forehead start to pulse. "I didn't need any time!" she shouted. "I didn't sleep with anyone but you. How could you accuse me of something like that after what happened with Jeff? I would never ever…" Claire's voice drifted off as though she couldn't even finish the sentence.

Luca knew that accusing her of having an affair was the lowest of low blows, but what other option was there? This wasn't a star in the east.

"You know, I'm not Jessica. I understand all that must've been awful for you, but don't take what she did out on me. This is totally different."

"Is it?" Luca asked. He wanted it to be different, but he wouldn't allow himself to entertain such a wild fantasy. He and Claire were through. It pained him, but there was no going back now. He needed to make a clean break and send her on her way before things got even uglier than they already were.

"Maybe you're right," he agreed with bitterness leeching into his voice. "Jessica was happy with just having one of my children. You're pushing for two. Wasn't having one of my kids enough? You had to get more out of me?"

Claire tried not to physically react to his insult. Now she wasn't just a slut, she was a greedy one? Where had this dark side of Luca hidden over the past few weeks? She thought he was holding back, but she never dreamed that *this* was what he'd kept from her. "More what? Money? I don't need your money, Luca."

His jaw tightened as he looked her over. "Then what's behind it? Afraid I might leave you once we got home? Did you think having a second miracle child would convince me to marry you so we could have a happily-ever-after?" He crossed his arms over his chest, challenging her to say otherwise.

She wasn't quite sure how to respond. This whole conversation had gone off the rails and there was no way to recover it. "I will admit that I'd hoped we could have a happily-ever-after with our two children, but there's no scheming involved. It simply is what it is."

"Claire, the only thing this is, is over. I knew it was a bad idea to seduce you, but you and your sad eyes and luscious lips convinced me otherwise. I don't know why I thought that us being together was the best resolution to our situation. Well, no more. You and I are through."

A sharp pain struck Claire's chest like Thor's hammer, radiating outward. She was certain it was the feeling of her heart breaking. How could she have loved a man who could be so cruel? She didn't really know him at all. All his smooth words and charming smiles had completely disarmed her.

"I thought we really had something special between us, Luca. But if you—" Her voice cracked with emotion as she fought to hold back tears. She didn't want him to see her cry. "If you are willing to accuse me of something that terrible and then cast me aside so easily, then I was wrong. About everything."

"I'm sorry to disappoint you."

His arrogant, ambivalent tone made her angry. It was one thing for him to be so convinced that he didn't believe her without proof. It was another to be downright cruel. She wasn't going to let another man treat her like less than she deserved. Luca was the one who taught her that, ironically enough.

Claire gathered up all her nerve, straightening her spine and looking him hard in the eyes like she had that first day at his lawyer's office. "You're only disappointing yourself, Luca, because you're a coward."

"A coward?" He nearly roared the words at her, but she refused to take a single step back.

Instead, she moved closer. "Yes, a coward. You're too scared to go to the doctor and find out the truth about your sterility. You'd rather throw away everything we have, accuse me of being a whore and a liar than face the reality of your condition."

"Why would I be scared to do that? The worst they can tell me is what I already know."

"No, it's not. The worst thing they can tell

you is that you've been wrong all this time. Because then you'd have to come to terms with the fact that you've been living half a life for all these years for no reason. You'd know for certain that you wasted over a decade where you could've found someone to love and started a family instead of being Mr. Busy CEO all the time. You've been hiding behind your desk instead of living your life."

Luca raised his arm, pointing toward the front door. "You take your venomous lies and get out of here before I call security and have you thrown out."

"You couldn't force me to stay one minute longer." Claire turned on her heel and marched back to the entryway where she scooped up her coat. "Since you're so certain this child isn't yours, I'm going to presume that you won't be dragging me to family court to get custody of this one."

"Nope," he snapped. "Not interested."

Claire tried not to react to his indifference. Not because of herself, but because of her child. She already felt a sense of protectiveness for it. The last thing she wanted was for the baby to feel as if the father didn't love it from the day they found out he or she existed.

"Fine. Then do me a favor and try not to be interested in Eva, either. If you don't want both your children, we don't want or need you in our lives at all," Claire said.

She flung open the front door and marched out, slamming it behind her with all the Mama Bear fury she could muster. It wasn't until she'd gotten on the elevator and the doors had safely shut that the anger subsided. With it gone, a rush of tears she couldn't stop flowed free.

How could she have gotten exactly what she wanted and lost everything she needed at the same time?

A beam of sunlight came through the window and shone across Luca's face. It roused him from his uncomfortable position on the leather couch in his living room. After a furious battle with a bottle of Scotch, he'd passed out there the night before.

He pushed himself up to a seated position and winced as the movement sent a sharp pain through his head. Bending over, he clutched his forehead and groaned. It was like a vise was clamped down on his skull, turning tighter with every movement and sound.

As pieces of the night before came back to him, he realized that even the agony of his head was miniscule in comparison to the ache of loss and disappointment that had settled in his chest.

Their angry words echoed in his head. The positive pregnancy test, the hopeful, the devastated, then the angry expressions on Claire's face, and then the slamming door flipping through his mind like a broken slide projector.

When he finally looked up, he spied the shattered remains of his cell phone. After Claire left, he'd reached for the closest thing he could lay his hands on and chucked it at the closed door of his apartment. He'd felt little satisfaction as his cell phone collided with the door and splintered across the marble entryway floor. Today, on top of everything else, he'd need to contact his assistant and have her order him a new phone.

With a curse, he leaned back against the couch and stared up at the ceiling. He'd lost it last night. That was very unlike him. He was always so in control, but Claire's betrayal had pushed him over the edge. After she left, all he could hear was his blood rushing through his veins; all he could see was tainted with the red hue of his emotions.

His child! She claimed to be pregnant with his child. Luca could hardly believe it when the words came out of her mouth. Not even the pregnancy test could convince him. How could he trust Claire's declaration that it was his baby? He couldn't. Not when he knew that it was impossible.

But did he *really* know?

As usual, morning and sobriety had brought everything into question. Not even the Scotch could drive Claire's words from his mind. She'd called him a coward because he hadn't been tested in all these years. He'd never really looked at it that way. Why did getting a slip of paper from the lab make a difference? It was just the final nail in the coffin he couldn't bear to seal. The radiation treatments destroyed his chances of fathering a child. End of story. It didn't matter how much he might want another child or how badly he wanted to believe her.

She had to know that he wanted another child. There was no other reason why she would come to him with a story like that. She'd found his weakness and did her best to exploit it.

Even as the thought rolled around in his foggy, hung-over brain, Luca knew it was wrong. Everything he'd said or done last night was contrary to what he knew to be true about Claire. It was like a monster had been unleashed inside him the moment she tested his beliefs. Once it got out, there was no stopping the flow of vile words from his mouth.

Disgusted with himself, he pushed up from the couch and stumbled into the kitchen to make a cup of coffee. That would help clear his thoughts, even if he feared it would make him realize his actions last night were that much more despicable.

He busied himself with his chore and sat down at the breakfast bar. Staring at the tile backsplash, he remembered the topic of Jessica coming up. He had tried and tried to put that whole situation out of his mind. That was why he hadn't told Claire about it at first. Of course, his mother didn't have any problem with sharing. Had the story his mother told her inspired Claire to come up with the lie about the baby? Or had the past simply poisoned his view of the present?

One thing he knew was that Claire was right when she said she wasn't Jessica. He knew that even as he accused otherwise. The two women were nothing alike. Jessica had been smart, but ambitious. They'd been compatible in bed, but he knew she wanted more. He'd wanted it, too, at first, but reality sunk in and he realized he'd never give her the family she wanted. So he'd retreated. "More" wasn't on the table. He ignored her texts and calls for a few months and finally she faded from his life. Until she showed up at the door very pregnant with "his" baby.

In the end, it had all been a hurtful lie. She wanted Luca back, wanted him to marry her. Apparently she wanted it badly enough to poke holes in all the condoms they used together, not knowing he was sterile. When that didn't work, she deliberately got pregnant by an Italian guy she met at a bar right after they broke up in the hopes she could pass it off as Luca's. It was incomprehensible. He never would've thought Claire would stoop to Jessica's level.

That's when the sobering thought crossed his mind—she wouldn't.

Claire believed what she was saying, whether it was true or not. But Claire had also told him she hadn't been with a man since Jeff. That didn't leave a lot of options, although it certainly explained the confused and betrayed look on her face when he rejected the idea of the baby being his.

He couldn't help it, though. That baby couldn't be his. It just couldn't.

But if it was...he'd made a huge, inexcusable and maybe unforgivable mistake.

Eleven

"Moretti?"

Luca looked up from his brand-new smart-phone when the nurse called his name. His stomach ached with dread. This was a moment he'd avoided for ten years. He'd almost called and canceled this appointment three times. The only reason he didn't was because he knew he'd have to face Gavin eventually.

His friend had listened sympathetically while he told him his sad tale. But instead of taking his side, he'd surprised Luca by pretty much saying the same things Claire had said. That he was a chicken. That his hurtful accusations were unfounded. Gavin had finished the conversation by telling him he needed to visit the doctor. Until he was tested and knew for certain that the baby couldn't be his, he needed to hold his tongue. He'd already said a lot he'd regret if he was wrong.

Luca knew Gavin was right, but that didn't mean he had to like it. Instead, he'd scheduled an appointment and that's where he found himself. Putting his phone away, he stood and followed the nurse down the corridor.

First, Luca was taken to a private room to produce a specimen for testing. When he was finished, he left the cup in the window and was led to an examination room to wait for the doctor.

It was an agonizing wait. He watched every minute tick by, the sense of anxiety growing with each second. At last, a soft knock came at the door and the doctor stepped inside with his file. It was the moment he'd dreaded and avoided since he'd finished his radiation treatments. Now he would know for certain if he was really the damaged man he'd always believed himself to be.

The doctor shook his hand and sat down on the tiny rolling stool. "Mr. Moretti," he began, flipping through the pages. "We have done a quick preliminary test of your sample. We're going to send it out to the lab for more detailed analysis, but I'm comfortable at this point with telling you that you are, in fact, able to have children."

Luca froze in disbelief. This was not what he'd expected at all. "Are you sure?"

"I'm not saying it will be as easy to impregnate a woman as it is for men without your medical history. Your sperm counts are lower than they would've been before your treatments, but you do still have motile, well-formed spermatozoa. With the right mix of circumstances, you can absolutely have children."

Luca wasn't sure what to say. He sat dumbfounded on the examination table as the doctor's words ran though his brain again and again.

"If you find you're having difficulty conceiving with your partner, a fertility clinic could be of some assistance."

Luca chuckled low and shook his head. "I'm through with fertility clinics, but thanks for the suggestion."

The doctor narrowed his gaze at Luca. "I'm not sure what that's about, but do you mind if I ask why you were tested today if not to start a family?"

Luca looked down at his hands. "Apparently I've already started a family. I didn't think it was a possibility, but it seems the right mix of circumstances happened."

The doctor's white eyebrows drew together in concern. "I'd say congratulations, but you don't seem very excited about the prospect of father-hood."

"It's not fatherhood that bothers me," Luca admitted. "I'm thrilled by the idea of it, even though I still run the risk of my cancer return-ing someday. I'll face that if it happens. It's just that I'm going to have a lot of apologizing to do to the baby's mother."

"Ahh," the doctor said, closing his file and setting it aside. "Well, if you want to know for certain, a blood test for paternity can be conducted even early on in the pregnancy."

Luca shook his head vehemently. Edmund would probably want that, but after everything he'd said to Claire, he couldn't ask her for that. He had no real reason to believe she was lying about the baby aside from the fact that he'd thought it to be impossible. They'd hardly left each other's side for weeks; she hadn't had the opportunity to meet and seduce another man. Now that he knew otherwise, there was no doubt.

Claire was pregnant with his child. And he was an ass.

"Okay, then I think we're done here unless you have any other questions. Good luck with your situation." The doctor stood and shook Luca's hand again. Just as quickly as he'd arrived, the doctor slipped out the door, leaving Luca alone with his thoughts.

He could have children. The old-fashioned way.

The idea had never really occurred to him. The

oncologists had been so doom and gloom about his prospects that he'd presumed the worst. Then he'd presumed the worst about Claire.

Claire. The woman who had been so mistreated by her husband that she had been loath to trust him or anyone else. The woman who had accepted him as he was. The woman who hadn't pushed him to talk about his past even as she struggled with her husband's dishonesty. The mother of his child. His *children*.

He'd treated her terribly. Luca never thought he could be so cruel to someone he cared about, and yet the harsh words had rolled off his tongue. Hopefully, the apology would come just as easily.

Luca sleepwalked through the motions of checking out of the doctor's office and making his way toward his apartment. Truthfully, he should've been calling for a car to take him back to the office, but he needed a little time to process all of this. That meant time away from his family. None of them knew where he'd gone or what had happened with Claire after they left Martha's Vineyard, but they would know something was wrong if they saw him right now. He was certain that shock and heartache were etched all over his face.

Stopping at a streetlight, Luca looked up and saw the Brooks Express Shipping building just ahead. Gavin would be expecting an update, so he might as well go on in and give it to him directly. Maybe he'd have a suggestion on how to make it up to Claire after everything he'd said and done.

In the lobby, he dialed Gavin and waited for his answer.

"Do you realize you've called me three times in the past month or so? I'm starting to feel special."

Luca sighed. "I'm in your lobby. Are you in?"

"I am. I've got a meeting in a half hour, but for now, I'm all ears."

Luca took the elevator up to the floor where Gavin's office was. He waved at his receptionist, blowing past her desk and into Gavin's office before she could stop him.

Gavin turned from his computer with an expectant look on his face. "So? Can your boys swim?"

Luca had to laugh at the way his friend phrased such a delicate question. "Yes, they can. They won't be winning any medals, but they can make it across the pool."

"Congratulations! Sit down." Gavin pointed to his guest chair as he got up from his own. "This calls for a celebration." He wandered over to his wet bar and poured two glasses of dark honey colored liquor.

Luca sat, eyeing his friend's desk. It was decorated with photographs from his wedding to Sabine, him holding his daughter, Beth, for the first time, all four of them on a plane, then on a beach. It made Luca want that. He wanted to litter his desk with family photos. But something kept holding him back.

Gavin carried the glasses back to the desk and handed one to Luca. Frowning at his friend, he said, "What's the matter? You look less than enthusiastic about the news."

Luca sipped the drink and winced at how strong it was. He wasn't much for Scotch, especially after overdoing it the other night. "I'm happy. Really, I am. But knowing the truth makes my fight with Claire that much worse. I've got to get her back somehow, but I don't know if she'll forgive me after what I said."

"Do you love her?" Gavin asked.

Luca nodded without hesitation. He hadn't actually thought about it, but the minute Gavin asked, the answer popped into his head as clear as day. Claire was unlike any woman he'd ever met. Since the day of their fight, he'd walked around with an aching hole in his chest. He missed her. He missed Eva. Now he even missed their baby growing inside her. He hadn't been around to take Claire to the doctor, listen to Eva's heartbeat or supply her with her strange cravings the first time. If he didn't get this fixed, he would lose his second chance at having the full fatherhood experience.

"I am madly, desperately in love with her,

Gavin." Saying the words aloud made him feel better and worse at the same time.

"Okay." Gavin's brows knit together in thought. "So tell me why you're in my office telling *me* this instead of on Claire's doorstep telling her?"

Luca supposed he could go to the museum right now and track her down, but he still had reservations. "It's not that simple. I've never let myself feel this deeply for anyone before. I always felt like I was a broken toy that no one would want, so I never even let myself have the dream of something like that."

Gavin just shook his head. "You're a fool, is what you are. You're a successful guy. You're handsome enough."

"Thanks," Luca said dryly.

"My point is that you're a great catch. Even with one testicle."

Luca ignored his friend's jesting slight. "I'm not a catch. I'm a time bomb. So what if I tell Claire I love her? What if she forgives me and we get married and have the baby together? What if I do all that and my cancer comes back? She's already been a widow once. I can't be responsible for her going through that a second time."

"You can't live your whole life waiting to die, man. You've got to get out there and start living. Anything can happen to any one of us. I could get hit by a cab or have an aneurism and drop dead at my desk with no warning at all. You've been in remission a long time. Stop letting your former illness hold you back. If you don't go to her, you've virtually left her a widow anyway—she's raising your children alone."

"And what if she'd rather be alone than be with me?"

"Then that is her choice. You can't make other people's decisions for them. I went years without Sabine because she decided we weren't a good fit. I never would've let her walk out that door if it had been my choice. But you've at least got to give her the opportunity to choose."

Gavin was right. Luca knew he was right. He just had to take all these old anxieties and put them aside. If the cancer came back, it came back. At least this time he would have Claire and the children to give him a reason to fight even harder.

He still didn't think he could march up to her and get a warm reception, however. He needed to open with a grand gesture. Not just jewelry or another flashy gift. It had to be something that would mean more than anything to her.

There was nothing in the world more important to Claire than Eva. Luca knew what he had to do. Taking another burning sip of his drink, he reached for his phone and called his lawyer.

Claire climbed the stairs of her brownstone with a heavy heart and even heavier limbs. She wasn't very far along in this pregnancy, but it was already wearing her out. That, combined with a return to her routine after a month away, left her thoroughly exhausted.

Yes, that was it. It wasn't the crushing oppression of heartache that was slowing her down.

Opening the front door, she found Daisy and Eva playing on the floor in the living room. Her nanny immediately stood and went over to give

Claire a hug. "Hey, Mama. How did the doctor's appointment go?"

Claire reached into her purse and pulled out the roll of sonogram pictures. There wasn't much to see, just a blurry little blob that looked something like a jelly bean. The first time she'd seen that image of Eva, her heart had nearly exploded with love and excitement. She and Jeff were finally going to be parents. This time the sight just made her sad. She would adore this baby, she had no doubt, but she couldn't help but think that she was once again having a child without a father around to love it the way it deserved to be loved. Was a mother's love enough? She hoped so.

Daisy snatched the photos out of her hand and gave a little squeal of excitement. "Congratulations. This is so exciting. I can't believe after how hard you worked to have Eva that you could get pregnant so easily."

Claire nodded absently, but she wasn't really listening. For the past week and a half, she'd been almost sleepwalking through her days. She certainly wasn't sleeping at night. She couldn't concentrate. All that ran through her mind again and again were the horrible things Luca had said to her.

"So I was thinking if we coated Eva in some flour, we could pan fry her and she'd come out with a nice crispy crust."

"Sounds good," Claire said automatically.

"Claire!" Daisy shouted in consternation. "You're not listening at all."

"I am," she argued.

"And what did you just agree to?"

Claire sighed and shook her head. "I have no idea."

"Sit down," Daisy demanded, pointing toward the couch.

She didn't feel like arguing, so she did as she was told. Daisy sat beside her, Eva playing with soft blocks on the floor in front of them.

"Just a tip, you might not want to agree to anything while you're in this state," Daisy said. "Now tell me what's going on? This isn't plain ol' pregnancy brain, is it?"

Claire opened her mouth to answer, but before she could say a word, the tears rushed to her eyes and all that came out was a strangled sob. Daisy hugged her to her chest, letting her get all the pain and heartache out of her system. It took several minutes and a soaked-through blouse, but eventually Claire was able to sit up, wipe her eyes and tell her sad tale.

"He doesn't believe the baby is his. I don't know how he could say that. I've spent the past month alone with him. Whose baby could it be?"

"I think he'll come around," Daisy said, holding her hand reassuringly. "Like you said, it sounds to me like he's spent too many years thinking that it could never happen. To believe he's the father means that everything he knows is wrong. If he's thrown away the past ten years of his life, too afraid to fall in love and disappoint his wife, it's got to be a serious blow. It's easier to push you away with angry accusations than to face the fact that he was too chicken to find out if he was sterile all this time."

Claire listened with a slow nod, but she wasn't

convinced that Luca would realize he was wrong. Luca was stubborn, and that same stubbornness might keep him from finding out the truth and admitting he was wrong. It might take a court mandated paternity test after the baby was born to convince him of the truth. At that point, he could apologize until he was blue in the face and it wouldn't make a difference. She didn't know if she could forgive him for how he'd treated her.

"The worst part is that I let myself fall in love with him, Daisy. It was so stupid of me. He just seemed to know how to get past every barrier I had. It had been so long since I felt like a man really cared for me. I must've been desperate for affection. Look where it got me…pregnant and alone."

"You are not alone, Claire." Daisy clasped Claire's chin and turned her so she was forced to look at her. "You've got me. You've got Eva. You've got this new baby. We're going to make this work, with or without this deadbeat billionaire."

"How?" It seemed like a ridiculous question

to ask, but she felt so bogged down in all of this, she could hardly come up with an answer.

"I'm going to move in," Daisy declared. "I'm going to be your live-in nanny to help take care of both the children. We are two strong, smart, capable women. We will be just fine without a man. Frankly, we only need them to start the baby process, after that they're kinda useless."

Claire chuckled, wiping away the last of her tears. "You're right. We will be just fine. No matter what happened between Luca and me, I'm coming out of this with another beautiful baby. I never dreamed I could ever have another, so I need to start thinking about this as the blessing that it truly is."

"That's the spirit," Daisy said with an encouraging tone. "Now, there's a roast chicken and vegetables in the oven for your dinner. Eva has already eaten her dinner and had her bath, so you two can take it easy tonight. Eat, relax and try not to beat yourself up too much about all this. I'll see you in the morning, okay?"

Claire nodded. "Thank you for the pep talk, Daisy. You deserve a raise."

Daisy laughed as she got up off the couch. "I'll remind you of that when you write my next pay-check." She walked over to the front door, slipping on her coat and waving good-night.

When the door clicked shut, Claire took a deep breath and tried to do what Daisy had told her to do. She scooped up Eva off the floor and carried her into the kitchen. She placed her in her swing and set it to a soothing rhythm the baby liked best. That kept her daughter occupied long enough for Claire to remove supper from the oven and make herself a plate.

Pulling up a stool at the breakfast bar, she took a few bites of chicken and started sorting idly through the stack of mail Daisy had left there for her. Bill, junk, bill… She stopped when she noticed the notepad that Daisy used to leave messages about phone calls.

Stuart, her attorney, had called. She'd had a missed call on her cell phone while she was at her doctor's appointment, but it had come at a critical time and then she'd forgotten to check it later. Searching through her purse, she found her phone and she was right. Her screen declared she'd missed a call from Stuart Ewing. She pressed the button to listen to the voicemail message.

"Claire, this is Stuart. I really need you to call me back tonight. It doesn't matter what time. There's been a development."

He left his personal number for her to call him. Claire's hand was shaking as she copied the number onto Daisy's notepad. She wished he hadn't been so vague in his message. "A development" could be anything. It could be that Luca decided to backpedal on their agreement and sue for full custody. She didn't think a judge would go along with that, but she couldn't be sure. The last time she saw Luca he'd been angry enough to do almost anything. Would he try to take Eva knowing she was the only thing Claire had? Just to spite her?

She had to stop speculating and just call Stuart back. She was going to make herself crazy if she didn't.

"Claire," Stuart said as he answered the phone. "Thanks for calling me back. We've received a request to meet with Luca and his lawyer tomorrow morning."

"Do we know if it's good or bad news?"

"I have no idea. I wasn't really expecting to hear from them when I did. Do you have any thoughts? How did the trip with Mr. Moretti go? I haven't spoken with you since you got back from Martha's Vineyard."

That was a loaded question. "It was a nice trip. I think we had everything worked out between us, so maybe it's just a finalization of our agreement to submit to the judge."

Stuart hesitated on the line. "What aren't you telling me, Claire? There's something about your tone that tells me you're leaving something out."

"Well, that's because I am. Things have gotten a little complicated since we left Martha's Vineyard, so I can't be certain that Luca will stick with the agreement we made." Claire could hear Stuart sigh heavily on the line.

"What happened when you got back?"

"I found out that I'm pregnant with Luca's child." She spit out the words as quickly as she could and waited for the fallout.

"Pregnant? I should've known you two going away together for a month would lead to trouble. Are you two an item, now? I hate to say it, but that would probably help the cause if you were."

"Not anymore," Claire admitted, dashing her lawyer's hopes. "He didn't take the news about the baby very well. He stated pretty bluntly that he didn't think it was his and got quite angry about the whole thing. So like I said, I don't have any clue what we'll face tomorrow."

"You know, I've been thinking over the past year about retiring. You may be the client that puts me over the edge."

At that, Claire had to laugh. She knew Stuart would work until he dropped dead in the court-room, but he was a curmudgeon about it anyway. "Look at it this way, Stuart—you just have to represent me in court. This is *my life*."

"You're right," he agreed. "I'll meet you at Edmund Harding's office at 8:45 a.m. tomorrow."

Twelve

"Are you sure you want to do this, Luca? You only have a few minutes left to change your mind."

Luca turned away from the window overlooking Central Park to gaze at his lawyer. "Yes. I have to do it."

"Actually, you don't," Edmund argued. He'd been irritated with Luca since he came in and started changing the arrangements they'd worked so hard to put together. "There's nothing that says giving up custody is the punishment for being mean to the mother."

"I'm not giving up custody," Luca argued. "I'm just setting the terms that will make her happiest. It's the least I can do after everything else."

"And what about you? What will make you happy? These are your children we're talking about. The children you never thought you'd have, I might add."

"Seeing Claire happy will make me happy," he answered without hesitation. It was true. As hard as this was on him, he needed to see Claire smile more than anything. That look of hurt and devastation on her face from that night at his apartment had haunted him for days. He was willing to do whatever it took to fix that, even giving up most of his rights to his children. He didn't want to do it, but it was the punishment he deserved after rejecting the baby as his own.

A soft knock came at the door and the receptionist stuck her head inside. "Mr. Harding, Mrs. Douglas and Mr. Ewing are here for your nine o'clock."

Edmund nodded sadly and looked at Luca. "Last chance."

Luca just waved away his concerns. He knew what he had to do, and he didn't care if his lawyer liked it or not.

"Send them in."

Luca took a seat at the table beside Edmund. For the first time in a long time, he felt nervous. He wasn't quite sure where to look as the door opened. He didn't know what he would see in Claire's eyes. Taking a breath, he looked up to see her as she slipped into the office behind her lawyer. Her gaze met his, and he knew that he was making the right decision. There wasn't the slightest hint of animosity there. She was anxious, exhausted, sad, but not angry. He had been the angry one, the one to lash out. She was just here to see what kind of punishment he was about to hand down because he thought she was lying to him.

They took their seats, and Luca squirmed slightly in his chair. Edmund eyed him suspiciously, but Luca ignored him. His focus was entirely on Claire. She didn't look good. He thought pregnant women were supposed to be radiant, but perhaps that was later on. Now she just looked run-down, like she had when he'd first taken her to Martha's Vineyard. A month of good food, sun and loving had changed her, but now it was like they'd never gone.

"Are you feeling okay?" he asked.

Everyone at the table, including Claire, looked startled. Edmund reached out to grip his forearm and silence him, but he pulled away. This wasn't about negotiations. It was about Claire.

Her gaze narrowed at him for a moment before she nodded. "I'm fine. I'm just having a rough first trimester. It was the same with Eva. Thank you for asking." Her tone was cold, and he deserved that.

"Mr. Harding, my client and I are curious what today's meeting is about. We go before the judge on Thursday. It's a little late to start making changes to the agreement that Mr. Moretti and Mrs. Douglas came to on their trip."

"I understand that," Edmund said. "As I'm sure you're aware, the agreement was made regarding Eva. The addition of a second child to the equation made it necessary for us to have another discussion."

"Wait a minute," Stuart said. "My understanding is that Mr. Moretti refused to acknowledge the child as his and vowed to Mrs. Douglas that he would not seek visitation. Are you saying that Mr. Moretti is acknowledging that Mrs. Douglas's second child is his, as well?"

"Yes, he is," Edmund replied.

Luca's gaze was set on Claire's face as his lawyer delivered the news. Her gray eyes widened with surprise, then she turned to him with her mouth agape. He could only nod, hoping his contrite expression let her know just how sorry he was about all of this.

"Is Mr. Moretti requiring any kind of testing to confirm the paternity of this child?" Stuart continued.

"No, he is not." Edmund's irritation was clear in his voice.

Stuart sat back in his chair, completely deflated by the whole situation. Apparently, they had come here expecting a battle and were caught off guard. Luca watched Claire's lawyer lean into her and say a few words. They quietly conversed for a moment with Claire's eyes meeting his a time or two.

"I'm sorry," Stuart said at last. "The last time our clients spoke, it was very clear that Mr. Moretti believed the child was not his. While we appreciate that your client is no longer accusing Mrs. Douglas of lying, may we ask what caused the sudden change of heart?"

Edmund turned to look at Luca. His lawyer had been strongly opposed to sharing Luca's private medical information with the other side, but Luca insisted. He nodded and Edmund took a deep breath. "Mr. Moretti has undergone medical testing to confirm his previous diagnosis. It was determined that he is a valid candidate for fathering Mrs. Douglas's second child."

Claire's mouth dropped open. There was a momentary light of excitement in her eyes, as though she wanted to congratulate him on the amazing news. The light dimmed quickly. She already knew he could have children, considering she was pregnant. The only thing that had changed was that he acknowledged it, as well.

Stuart ignored both clients, trying to focus on the confusing negotiations. "Now that Mr. Moretti is acknowledging the child, how does this change the custody agreement?"

Edmund slid the folder of paperwork across the table with their updated agreement. "You can take your time looking it over. We presume that your client will find these new terms acceptable."

Luca watched as Claire and Stuart reviewed the paperwork, talking quietly between one another. It was agonizing to sit silently and watch as Claire shook her head and her gaze flickered curiously over him from time to time.

He wasn't entirely sure what was taking them so long to make a decision. He had given Claire everything she wanted. He'd granted her sole physical and legal custody of the children. He'd asked for minimal visitation, less than half of what they'd agreed to, as to not cause an interruption to the children's routines. He'd tripled the amount of requested child support—even though he knew she wasn't interested in his money— and offered to pay for the private schooling of her choice. He'd even set up large, generous trust funds for both of the children. What more could she possibly want? He didn't want to walk away entirely or the children would think he didn't care about them. He did. More than anything. There was a fine line between giving Claire what she wanted and abandoning his children.

Finally, Stuart shook his head. "I'm sorry, but this offer is unacceptable. My client wants more."

Claire watched Luca's expression crumble at her lawyer's declaration. She knew it was a risk, but it was one she had to take. Yes, the offer was everything she could've hoped for when they first started this process, but now everything had changed. It was missing once crucial element—Luca.

With what he was offering, she could easily raise the two children on her own. She could hire Daisy as a live-in nanny and even give her a bigger raise than she could ever afford on her own. They could attend the best schools in New York and have everything they ever wanted. Everything but a father.

"What do you want, Claire? Do you want me to open up a vein and bleed for you? Because I will."

It was the first time he'd spoken since he'd asked how she was. There was a pleading in his eyes that made her chest ache. It felt so awkward to have these legal mouthpieces between them. Everything felt so stiff and official with Edmund and Stuart doing all their talking for them. She wished she could just make the lawyers go away for ten minutes so they could talk—really talk—without all the legal protections in the way.

With them here, all she could do was lay her heart on the line and see if he bit. Luca had acknowledged this baby was his. This updated offer was as close to an apology as he probably knew how to offer. But she wanted more. He'd spent weeks telling her she was worth more than what Jeff had given her. She'd finally decided to believe him, and she was going to demand it.

"This isn't nearly enough. Your money doesn't mean a damn thing to me. I want you to apologize for all the terrible, hurtful things you said to me. I want you to say you're sorry for accusing me of sleeping with someone else and threatening to have security throw me out of the building. And then, when I'm satisfied, I want *you*, Luca."

His sharp gaze met hers for a moment. He swallowed hard, then adjusted his posture in his seat. "Gentlemen, may we have a moment alone?"

"Luca, I don't advise you to—"

"Alone," he reiterated in a firm voice that left no question of his demand.

Claire squeezed Stuart's hand reassuringly, and both men got up from the table. They made their way out, shutting the door behind them.

There were a few quiet, strained moments before Luca spoke. "I'm sorry, Claire."

She wanted to respond, but she held herself

back. With the lawyers gone, she wanted to know what he had to say.

"I'm not saying any of this because you're demanding it. I'm saying it because it needs to be said. You're totally right. I'm sorry I doubted you. I'm sorry I said all those horrible things. I just never believed that I…" His voice trailed off as he shook his head and looked down at the table. "For so long, I've felt incomplete. Having cancer robbed me of so much. Not just my childhood and my youthful sense of immortality, but my self-worth. My sense of safety."

Claire watched as he pushed up from the glass conference-room table and walked over to the window. "Everything you said that day was right. I was scared. I'd put off knowing the truth for so long because it left me a glimmer of hope. Once I knew for certain, it was done. But I went to the doctor after our fight."

He turned away from the view and looked at Claire. "I can have children. I never dreamed a doctor would tell me that, but he did. In that moment, I wasn't happy, though. I felt terrible because I knew that you didn't deserve any of the things I said to you that day."

Crossing the room in four long strides, he stopped in front of Claire. "Did you really mean what you said before? That you still want me after everything I've said and done?" Luca dropped onto one knee in front of her and scooped her hands into his own.

Claire felt her chest tighten with each word he said. "I meant every word. I don't want your money, Luca. I never have. And I do appreciate your offer of giving me full custody of the children. I know that's a huge gesture for you. But it's just not enough. I want my children to have a father. I want them to have you in their lives."

Luca's posture relaxed, and his dark gaze fell to their intertwined fingers. "And what about you? Do you want me in your life, too, Claire?"

At that, Claire sighed. She'd gone over this a thousand times in her mind. Should she be happy to have a child and some good memories from her time with Luca? Did she dare ask for more? Was more even possible? "I don't know.

A lot of that depends on you. A very smart man once told me that a woman is a gift to be cherished. I've spent far too long being treated as less than enough. I'll want you in our children's lives no matter what, but to be in mine, I want it all. I'm not going to settle this time, or ever again."

Luca nodded slowly. "I don't want you to settle. I've never wanted a woman to settle for me, and I don't want you to have anything less than you deserve. Selfishly, I'll tell you that I love you, Claire. The time we've spent apart has been agonizing. I absolutely want our children to play a part in my life, but I'll be honest when I say it will kill me to see you every time we pass the children from one household to the other. It's not at all what I want. I want us to be a family, together, but I'm worried."

"About what?"

"I'm worried that I'm going to get sick again. I know I shouldn't let it affect my decisions and how I live my life, but I need you to know that it's a real possibility. If you can accept that and want us to be a family, okay. If losing you is the price I pay for my sins, I accept that, too."

"Sins?" Claire's eyes were overflowing with tears as she listened to him speak. He was already punishing himself far more harshly than she ever would have. "You haven't committed any sins, Luca. You've just been hurt. We've both been hurt. We let that disappointment get between us. We can't let that happen again."

A spark of hope glimmered in Luca's eyes as he looked up at her. "Does that mean there's a chance of us being a 'we' again?"

Claire nodded through her tears. "I love you too much to just walk away."

A wide grin broke out across Luca's face, making her chest ache. She couldn't help returning the smile. "You love me?"

"I do."

Luca looked up at her with a suddenly serious expression. "We're in love, you're having my baby and I'm already down on one knee. I guess there's just one thing left to do, Claire."

She stiffened in her seat at his words. Did

he mean what she thought he meant? Was he actually…?

"Claire Marianne Lawson," Luca began, "you came into my life in the most unexpected of ways and you gave me the greatest gift I could ever imagine—our beautiful little Eva. Being with you has been some of the happiest times of my life. Every day I want to get out of bed and find a way to make you smile. I want to do that for the rest of my life. Will you allow me to do that by giving me the honor of becoming my wife?"

Before she could respond, Luca reached into his pocket and pulled out a small, velvet box. He lifted the lid, and Claire found a beautiful oval diamond solitaire inside. On one side was a round, dark blue sapphire. On the other was a lighter blue stone.

"The sapphire is for Eva, since she was born in September," he explained. "The blue topaz is for the new baby. By my calculations, he or she should arrive in late December. If I'm wrong and the baby doesn't show up until January, we'll change it to a garnet."

Claire's eyes blurred with tears to the point that she couldn't make out the details anymore. It didn't matter. It was the most perfect ring he ever could've given her. She didn't care how many carats it was or how much money he'd paid. It represented not only their commitment to each other, but their children. That made it the most precious piece of jewelry she could ever wear.

"Yes," she said at last, realizing she hadn't yet answered his very important question. "Yes, I will marry you."

Luca took the ring from the box and slipped it onto her finger. She glanced at it for only a moment before reaching out and pulling Luca's face to hers. Their lips met, giving her the thrill she craved more than a ring.

He didn't disappoint. Wrapping his arms around her waist, he stood up, pulling Claire out of the chair with him. She laced her fingers at his nape and pulled him closer to her. She couldn't get enough of him. She'd come far too close to losing his touch forever.

Finally, Luca pulled away, still holding her tight in his arms. "We'd better stop. I don't think Edmund would be too pleased with me making love to my fiancée on his conference-room table."

Claire beamed at his use of her new title. "Well," she argued, "considering how much *my* fiancé has paid for his services, we should be able to do whatever we'd like."

"Soon," he promised, planting another, shorter kiss on her lips. "We've just got to call off the dogs and I'll whisk you home and make love to you all afternoon."

"Before we go, I just have one question. How did you know my maiden name?" Claire asked as she looked up at him.

Luca gave her a sly smile. "You ran a background check on me, so I ran one on you. It's only fair, right?"

She smiled wide. "Absolutely. Did you find

out anything interesting while you were nosing around?"

"Just that you got a D in freshman chemistry, and your favorite food is listed on Facebook as Thai. Thai? Really?"

"I may need to update that," Claire admitted with a smile. "I'm pretty partial to Italian lately."

"You'd better be. So," he continued with a heavy sigh. "Are we ready to let the sharks know the good news?"

Claire nodded. "Let's get it over with so I can get you home and out of this suit."

"Edmund!" Luca shouted toward the conference-room door.

A moment later the door burst open with both lawyers standing anxiously in the doorway. They looked curiously at Luca and Claire, wrapped in each other's arms.

"Yes?"

"Withdraw the custody motion. We don't need to go to court." Luca kept his dark hazel eyes focused only on Claire as he spoke. Her heart fluttered in her chest when he looked at her that way.

"We don't?"

"No," Claire said with a sly smile. "We're headed to the wedding chapel instead."

Epilogue

July 4th
Martha's Vineyard

"It's not going to zip." Claire was in full-blown panic mode. The wedding started in less than a half hour and her blossoming belly and swelling bosom were causing a major issue with her dress.

"It's going to zip," Daisy assured her. "You did the final alteration a week ago. You haven't gotten that much bigger in the last week."

Claire held her breath as she felt Daisy tug and

groan slightly, then the rush of the zipper as it raced to the top. "Thank goodness," she said with a sigh of relief.

Her first wedding dress had been a princess extravaganza that made it impossible for her to use the restroom alone. This time, she'd opted for something more appropriate for the beach. It was strapless with a sweetheart neckline and a beaded bodice. The flowing organza gathered under the bust and draped to the floor. It was light and ethereal, yet sparkly enough to feel special. She loved it.

"Oh, Claire." Antonia Moretti came into the master bedroom of the cottage that was doubling as the bridal suite. "You look so beautiful. Luca will be beside himself when he sees you."

She hoped so. They had put together this wedding plan quickly, which made her nervous, but she didn't want to be eight months pregnant and huge in all their wedding pictures. Thankfully, most of it had come together easily. Gavin had offered the beach house at Martha's Vineyard as the wedding location. It was the perfect choice, since they'd fallen in love here. The wedding and reception was taking place on the beach with a roaring bonfire, a local band playing and a stellar fireworks show to wrap up the night. The seafood shack up the road was catering a traditional New England boil on the beach with loads of fresh clams, mussels, shrimp, spicy sausage, corn and potatoes.

That wasn't what Claire was looking forward to the most. She was anxious for the cake. Well, the cheesecake. They'd opted out of the traditional cake and brought in a dozen different cheesecakes from their nearest restaurant in Newport. Food hadn't been very kind to Claire's stomach for the first few months of her pregnancy, but she was finally getting her appetite back. She couldn't wait for Luca to feed her a bite of creamy cheesecake with fresh strawberries on top.

A soft tap sounded at the door. She almost didn't hear it over the chatter of Luca's sisters as they did their hair and makeup. Daisy opened the door and to Claire's surprise her mother was standing there with Eva in her arms.

"Mom?"

Her mother smiled and stepped into the room, looking so familiar, yet so different than she remembered. "Hello, Claire. Just look at you. You're even prettier than I ever dreamed."

Claire rushed over to hug the mother she hadn't seen since right after her marriage to Jeff. "I can't believe you made it."

"Living across the country, I might be horribly neglectful in many ways, but I'm not going to miss my only child's wedding. It's bad enough that this is the first time I've seen Eva." She placed a kiss on the baby's fat cheek. Eva was wearing a little white dress with a tulle tutu as the honorary flower girl. "That's all going to change, though. Your stepfather and I are moving to Connecticut next month. Plan on seeing me a lot more often," she added with a smile.

Claire could hardly believe it. She'd been content in gaining Luca's large, loud family as her own, but to have her mother close again made tears start to pool in her eyes. She looked up and breathed through her nose. If she messed up her eye makeup, Carla would get onto her.

"I hate to break up the family reunion," Daisy said, "but it's time to get this wedding going."

The Moretti sisters scrambled to gather their things and slip out of the room. Daisy was carrying Eva down the aisle, so she took her from her grandmother's arms. "Follow me and I'll have the ushers seat you."

Then, just as quickly, Claire found herself alone. She gave herself one quick glance in the mirror and picked up her bouquet. Her stomach was fluttering, but for the first time in weeks, it was just nerves, not nausea. She took a deep breath and the anxiety faded. There was no reason to be worried about this wedding. She'd never been more sure of anything in her life as she was about marrying Luca.

Glancing out the window, she saw all the parents seated and Daisy followed. It was time to go.

Stepping carefully downstairs, she stopped at

the deck to await her music. There, she could see several rows of white chairs lining the sandy path to the archway, filled with faces of friends and family, eager and happy to witness this moment. Beneath the archway of white flowers stood the officiant, Daisy, Eva and Luca.

His gaze was glued to her as she came outside. For once, it was his jaw that dropped open with amazement and his eyes that shone glassy with tears. He was wearing a white linen suit without a tie, keeping the look casual. Even then, he was still the most handsome man she'd ever seen in person. It was hard to believe this man—the father of her children—was about to be her husband. It was more than she ever could've hoped for.

The music started and everyone stood and turned to look in her direction. Claire stepped barefooted into the soft golden sand and headed down the path to her happily-ever-after.

* * * * *

MILLS & BOON®

Why shop at millsandboon.co.uk?

Each year, thousands of romance readers find their perfect read at millsandboon.co.uk. That's because we're passionate about bringing you the very best romantic fiction. Here are some of the advantages of shopping at www.millsandboon.co.uk:

* **Get new books first**—you'll be able to buy your favourite books one month before they hit the shops

* **Get exclusive discounts**—you'll also be able to buy our specially created monthly collections, with up to 50% off the RRP

* **Find your favourite authors**—latest news, interviews and new releases for all your favourite authors and series on our website, plus ideas for what to try next

* **Join in**—once you've bought your favourite books, don't forget to register with us to rate, review and join in the discussions

Visit **www.millsandboon.co.uk**
for all this and more today!